'AWESOME! My friend read it same thi... ...e, till some unearthly hou... ...ok is un-put-downable!'
Sarah

'It was as if Emily cou... ...like you'd written about me or anything, just the way she reacted to situations, especially the problems with her friends. I loved this book. The characters were extremely true to life, I was v... ...ry down.'
Samantha, 10

'It was uncomfortable at times for me to read, which indicates that you've hit the mark - there were definitely sections that could have come straight from my head. An excellent understanding of what goes on in a self-harmer's mind.'
Charlotte, 25

'From a first read through I thought it was amazing. There was an AWFUL lot of stuff in there that I could really relate to. Past the fact that it was my A-levels and not my GCSEs I screwed, she basically could have been me. To be honest it was interesting to read and it gave me some stuff to think about.'
Kirsty, 18

'All the scenes with her mother I read with bated breath as they reminded me exactly of the interaction between myself and my mother as a teen.'
Siân, 23

'It's stylish, polished and moving, told with real wit and insight.'
Kathryn Robinson, Literary Consultant for Cornerstones

'A very important, new type of book, written with great competence, flair and imagination. It's a terrific and powerful read but it will also help people.'
Ian Huish, psychotherapist

Red Tears

Joanna Kenrick

ff

faber and faber

First published in 2007
by Faber and Faber Limited
3 Queen Square London WC1N 3AU

Typeset by Faber and Faber Limited
Printed in England by Bookmarque Ltd

A CIP record for this book
is available from the British Library

ISBN 0–571–23483–6
ISBN 978–0–571–23483–7

2 4 6 8 10 9 7 5 3 1

acknowledgements

Thanks are due to many people, not least the members of the Bodies Under Siege online forum, who responded to my questions by writing accounts of their personal experiences. I feel very privileged that you shared your thoughts and feelings with me. I must particularly thank those members who read an early draft of the book and provided helpful (and in some cases extensive) feedback: Claire, Sarah, Charlotte, Zoë, Jennifer, Rebecca, Siân, Samantha and Kirsty.

I also had many responses from the members of the Lush International Forum, some of whom have personal experience of self-harm, and some of whom work in mental health. Thank you for helping me with my research.

Sincere thanks are due to two professionals: Sarah Fortune at the Centre for Suicide Research in Oxford, who talked me through what would happen at Accident and Emergency; and Ian Huish, a psychotherapist who actually conducted a therapeutic session with me playing the role of Emily. Much of the dialogue in Emily's therapy was lifted directly from that session.

Finally, I should like to thank Kathryn Robinson at Cornerstones Literary Consultancy and my agent Penny Holroyde, for their unwavering faith in the book; and my husband, Phillip Cotterill, for his constant support and encouragement.

Warning: If you are a self-harmer, you may find parts of this book triggering. Please take responsibility for your own safety.

prologue

I open the box.

Inside it is softness and steel. Tissues and blades.

I carefully remove a blade and lay it to one side. Then I take out six tissues and place them by my arm, ready.

I stretch out my left arm, examining it for a spare patch of skin. A patch not already marked by scars.

Then I pick up the blade.

In this moment, I am calm. I know what to do. The overwhelming feelings are suspended.

I draw the blade across my arm. Blood springs to the surface.

I sit back, watching the blood run down my arm before reaching for the tissues to prevent the blood from staining my clothes.

I dab at the wound, tenderly, caringly.

I feel so much better.

I know that tomorrow I will feel stupid. I will look at my arm and feel so disappointed in myself. I have let everyone down again.

I don't do this because I like it.

I do it because I don't know what else to do.

you're such a good friend, Emily Bowyer

'You mustn't worry so much,' I say. 'It's not as bad as you think.'

'Isn't it? What about when they find out I didn't do my Eng Lit assignment?' Lizzie pulls at her hair.

'Don't do that. You'll make your hair fall out.'

'And what about when they find out I'm still seeing Adam?'

'Oh Lizzie, didn't you tell them?'

She pulls a face. 'I'm not like you, Em. I can't talk to my parents. You're lucky, your parents are really cool.'

That's only because I don't have a boyfriend, I think. And I don't push my luck with my parents like Lizzie does.

'So what should I do?'

I put a hand on her arm. 'Look, it's going to be fine. Really. We don't have Eng Lit until Tuesday. I'll help you do it. They won't ever know.'

'And what about Adam?'

'I thought you didn't like him much anyway.'

'That was last week. He's been really sweet to me lately.'

I

'Liz, your parents are bound to find out at some point. Why don't you just invite him round and tell him to be on his best behaviour? Then your parents can see what a good judge of character you are.'

She grins. 'I love that idea. I can just see the look on Mum's face. Not sure Adam will like it, though.'

'Well, you'll just have to talk him round,' I say, starting to feel irritated. 'If he's serious about you, he'll just have to grit his teeth and make nice with your parents.'

She hugs me. 'You're such a good friend, Emily Bowyer. What would I do without you?'

'You'd be fine,' I say.

'I wouldn't. I'd fall apart without you to tell me what to do.'

'You'd have to think for *yourself*,' I say in mock horror.

'I *know*! Can you imagine how long that would take?'

I laugh. 'Well, at least your brain has had a nice six-week rest before the —'

'*Nightmare year*,' we say in unison.

'I'll make a bet with you,' says Lizzie. 'I bet you a Baileys Mini that the very first teacher we have today mentions GCSEs.'

'Oh, surely not,' I protest. 'We've only just come back. They wouldn't be that cruel.'

'This is school, Em,' says Lizzie. 'They train in cruel camps to teach here.'

As it turns out, she's right. First lesson is French.

'Now,' says Miss Collins, brushing the hair out of her eyes. I don't know why she doesn't tie it back; it gets on my nerves. 'As you are aware, this is possibly the most

2

important year of your young lives.' Lizzie raises her eyebrows at me.

'*She didn't say it,*' I mouth at her.

'We only have two terms before your GCSEs,' says Miss Collins.

'*You owe me,*' Lizzie mouths back.

'And because of that, I do not expect you to be carrying on your own conversations whilst I am talking,' says Miss Collins to Lizzie – who flashes a grin at me and straightens her face so she can look apologetic to Miss Collins.

I stifle a giggle and Marianne frowns at me. I don't care. She's too stuck up for her own good. She sits across from Lizzie and spends most of the time chewing gum and playing with her hair. I pretend to like her because Lizzie likes her, but really she gets up my nose.

Every single teacher that day mentions GCSEs, with the exception of Mr Hicks, our History teacher, who simply writes 'GCSE' on the board. 'I think you get the point,' he says.

I sure do.

By the end of the first week back, I am finding it hard to remember what holidays are like. We have so much homework it's unbelievable. 'How do they expect us to get through all of this?' Lizzie says, staring at the pile of folders and books on her desk. 'Do they think we don't have social lives?'

'I know,' I say. 'It's going to take me the whole weekend to get through it.'

'Oh, don't be daft, Em,' says Lizzie. 'You'll sail through it, you know you will. You always do. I wish I could just *do* stuff, like you. You hardly have to think about it.'

'What do you mean?'

Lizzie grins at me. 'Oh, come on. You don't have to work as hard as most people. You're just lucky like that. Must be that mega-brain in there.' She taps the side of her head.

'Mega-brain?' I say slowly. I sort of know what she means, but she's got it all wrong. I *do* have to work. It just doesn't always take me as long to figure out what I've got to do as other people. But the donkey work takes as long. She's laughing, so maybe it was just a joke. I laugh too. 'Yeah, mega-brain, that's me. Genius level. I don't even know what I'm doing at this school really. I should be at university by now.'

'Yeah, doing at least three degrees at once.'

'Are you kidding? I could be doing a right angle,' I joke.

Lizzie looks blank. 'Huh?'

'Ninety degrees,' I prompt. Comprehension flits over her face.

'Oh yeah, right.' She smiles, but I sense she's annoyed she didn't get the joke straightaway. Have I made her feel stupid? Or was it just a really lame joke? Trying to be too clever.

'Are you coming over this weekend?' I say as we walk out of the school gates.

Lizzie pulls a face. 'Sorry, can't. I'm going swimming with Marianne on Saturday, and Mum says we've got to have a family meal on Sunday. Don't know why, we never talk to each other.'

'Oh.' I wait for her to invite me swimming too, but she doesn't. 'See you Monday, then.'

'Yeah.' She smiles and waves before getting into her mum's car. 'See you.'

Is she punishing me for making her feel stupid? I shouldn't have made that joke about right angles; she probably thinks I was showing off.

She has been seeing a lot of Marianne over the holidays.

Oh, shut *up*, Emily! You're just being paranoid!

I walk to the bus stop, feeling the straps of my bag digging into my shoulder. I had forgotten what it's like to carry a ton of books around. When I reach the stop, I put my bag on the ground with relief. There's a new girl there today. I know most of the girls in my year, but I haven't seen this one before. She must be in Year Eleven, though, because she's carrying the same textbooks as me. I smile and sit down on the bench. She smiles back. We don't say anything.

On Monday, Lizzie suddenly runs up to me. 'Em, you've got to help me!'

'What's the matter?'

'That essay! The one that's due in tomorrow – the Eng Lit one.'

'Lizzie, don't tell me you still haven't done it!'

'You said you'd help me.'

'Well, yes, but I haven't seen you all weekend, so how could I?'

Lizzie looks hurt. 'Don't be like that, Em; it's not my fault I was busy.'

But it's your fault you went swimming with Marianne and not with me, I think, and banish the thought immediately. What a nasty thing to think. Stop being spiteful, Emily.

'What do you want me to do?' I ask.

'Come round tonight. Pleeeease! I don't even know what to write about.'

'But you've read the book, haven't you?'

She looks guilty. I am horrified. 'You haven't even read the book! Lizzie, what were you thinking? How can you possibly write an essay on a book you haven't read!'

Lizzie scrapes her foot on the tarmac. 'I was hoping . . .'

She wants me to write it for her. But that's cheating. Isn't it?

'Look,' she says desperately. 'You know there's no one else I can ask. And you don't have to write it for me, you just have to explain it to me and then I can write it myself. Honest.' She bats her eyelashes at me, and I laugh uneasily.

'Oh, all right.' I know this is a bad idea, but what can I say? She's my best friend. And she's right, there isn't anyone else she can ask. 'I'll be round at seven, OK?'

'Make it six and come for dinner,' Lizzie says promptly. 'Then you can talk to my parents and I don't have to.'

When the bell goes at the end of the day I wish more than ever that I'd said no to Lizzie. I have two homeworks due in tomorrow, one for Thursday and one from the weekend that I haven't finished yet. When am I going to do them?

'See you later,' says Lizzie, skipping off. I watch her get into the car enviously. I wish my mum would come and pick me up instead of my having to get the bus. But she doesn't get in from work until after me.

The new girl isn't at the bus stop today. The bus is crowded, though, and I manage to sit on a piece of chewing gum which sticks to my skirt. Mum will kill me. I try to ignore the group of stupid boys who are comparing the latest computer games, and the group of girls who are bitching about someone they say is their friend. 'I mean, she's really sweet and everything, but she's just so – *pure*. Don't you think?'

I gaze out of the window and wonder if anyone talks about me that way. Sweet and everything, just so – what? Stupid? Annoying? Bad at jokes? I pinch myself on the leg in irritation. For God's sake, stop thinking about the stupid, stupid joke. It didn't mean anything. Lizzie's probably forgotten all about it by now. Can't you even get a grip on your own paranoia?

I let myself into the kitchen and make a cup of tea. Then I carry it upstairs to my room. My room – untidy, but I know where everything is. Blue carpet, slightly worn in the patch by my bed. Turquoise bedspread, three years old now but I still like the colour. Purple beaded lampshade from some stall in the market. White chest of drawers, slightly off-white wardrobe. Desk, covered in pencils, paperclips, scraps of paper and pen-pots.

I have three pen-pots, but I don't know why. I never put any pens in them.

I clear a space for my tea and drag my bag across the carpet. What shall I do first? Which homework will take the least time? Maths, probably. At least you don't have to do any thinking in Maths – you just work your way steadily through the questions.

I make a start on the Maths. About half an hour later, I hear Mum come in with Anthony. 'Emily?' she calls up.

'Yeah, I'm home,' I call back.

'Do you want a cup of tea?'

'No thanks.' I stare at the still-full cup of tea on my desk. 'I've already had one.' Why did I make a cup of tea anyway? I don't even *like* tea that much. I made it automatically, like my mum does. Are you feeling tired? Have a cup of tea. Bad day at school? Cup of tea, that's what you need. Fallen over and broken your leg? I know just what'll sort that out . . .

I glance at the clock and give a start. Five o'clock already. Where did the time go? I have to go out in half an hour!

Two pairs of feet thump up the stairs and Mum sticks her head round the door. 'Hiya. Everything all right?'

'Yeah,' I say. 'Mountains of work, though, don't know how I'm going to get it all done.'

'Well, you've got the whole evening.'

'I'm going round to Lizzie's for six.'

She frowns. 'What time will you be back?'

'Not sure – we're going to do our homework together.' Well, that's half true. We're going to do her homework anyway.

'Oh, I see.' She pauses for a moment. 'Does that mean you won't be here for dinner?'

'Yeah – sorry.'

'I don't mind, Emily, but I would appreciate a little more notice. We're having steak and chips, and now I'll have one steak left over.'

'Give it to Anthony. He's a growing boy, he needs the protein.'

'What's that?' My brother comes running into the room. 'Was that about me?'

'Yes, I said you need feeding up because you're too skinny,' I tell him.

Anthony's face falls. 'Am I? I'm not, am I, Mum?'

'No, of course you're not, silly.' She hugs him. 'Emily was making a joke, that's all.'

Bad Joke Emily, that's me. A bad joke for every occasion.

Anthony goes back to his room and Mum frowns at me. 'Try not to put him down.'

'I'm not!'

'He's got enough on his plate at the moment, what with starting a new school . . .' She looks behind her, then comes in and shuts the door. 'Does he seem different to you?'

'Different? What sort of different?'

She shakes her head. 'Oh, I don't know. He's been a bit quiet since the beginning of term, don't you think?'

'Er.' I haven't noticed.

'I mean, normally he'd be coming home and telling me everything that happened during the day. He hasn't done that at all. When I ask, he just says, "Oh, it was OK," and then clams up.'

I glance at the clock. Ten past five. My homework time is ebbing away. 'Maybe he's just growing up, Mum. He can't be that enthusiastic little boy for ever.'

She pulls a face. 'Maybe. I guess he won't always want to tell me everything that's going on in his life. I expected that he'd be bubbling over about the new school, though. Didn't you?'

'Well, perhaps he doesn't like it. Secondary school is a big step, Mum. He's probably just feeling a bit overwhelmed. He'll settle in soon.'

She sits on my bed. 'Do you think you could ask him how it's going? He'd tell you things he wouldn't tell me.'

I glance at the clock again. How long is this going to take? I only have nineteen minutes left to finish the Maths and do the Science – plus the English from the weekend. 'Er,' I say, but she interrupts me.

'You know how he looks up to you. And you've been through it recently. Not like me – he probably thinks I'm too old to understand.'

'Mum, don't you think you're getting a bit too worked up over nothing?' I say desperately. Hasn't she said all she needs to say?

She straightens out the creases in my duvet. 'I'm sure you're right. I worry too much, don't I?' She smiles at me suddenly. 'At least I don't have to worry about you. It's such a comfort, knowing you just get on with things. I'm really proud of you for the way you handle your work. Maybe I compare Anthony to you without realising – and that's wrong. He's a different person.'

'Yeah.' I glance at the clock again. Eighteen minutes.

She stands up. 'He'll talk to me when he's ready, won't he?'

'I'm sure he will.'

'It's a big change, like you said. From two hundred kids in the school to two hundred in his year. And not many of his friends went with him.'

'No.' I'm in one of those strange conversations where I only have to say 'yes' and 'no' alternately. For God's sake, Mum, *go away*. I only have seventeen and a half minutes and you need to get out of my room so I can get back to work.

'Anyway, we'll all be extra supportive, won't we? So that he feels he can talk to us at any time.'

'Yeah. Sure.'

Mum sighs. I grab the chance.

'Mum, I've really got to get on with this.'

She shakes her head. 'Of course, sorry. I've been rambling, I know. You're just so good at listening! I'll come and pick you up from Lizzie's at nine-thirty, OK?'

'Great, thanks.'

She finally leaves my room. I have seventeen minutes.

No way.

you always over-react

'Thank God you're here,' Lizzie says as she opens the door. 'They're at it again.'

She means her parents. I can hear them bickering in the kitchen. Her mum's voice is really high and sharp.

'Look, I don't see why you should be able to when I can't. I have friends too, you know.'

'Really? Where are they, then? If it was such a problem for you, you should have said at the time.'

'I did, but you weren't listening. You never listen.'

They bicker a lot. They don't even stop when they have visitors. I feel really weird when they argue in front of me. We don't argue much at my house – everything is sorted out logically, and we talk stuff through. My mum says arguing is unproductive. So I feel awkward when I go to Lizzie's and her parents argue.

'Let's go upstairs,' says Lizzie. 'Mum, Dad, Emily's here!' she yells as we make our way up to her room.

'Hi, Emily!' I hear floating up before they resume their bickering. I shake my head to dislodge the yucky feeling.

Lizzie's room is smaller than mine, but then she doesn't

have as much stuff. What she does have is a lot of posters. This band, that movie star, the other bloke off the telly. I don't know who they are half the time. I've had to force myself to listen to the charts since primary school so I can keep up with the conversations. I don't really like pop, I'm more into trancy stuff, music I can not-really-listen-to when I'm working.

'Oh, I've been meaning to ask you,' says Lizzie. 'Did you see that programme last week about plastic surgery? Gross!'

'No, I didn't,' I say. 'Any good?'

'It was *disgusting*,' says Lizzie with relish. 'They showed the actual operations – people having their stomachs cut open so they could get the fat out, all that kind of stuff.'

'Eww.'

She demonstrates on her own stomach, miming cutting it open with a large pencil and fat dribbling out. It's funny but I feel slightly sick at the same time. I've always had too much of an imagination – I can almost see the yellowy fat oozing out of her.

When she's finished her gruesome mime, she bounces off the bed. 'I bought some new nail varnish the other day. Want to do yours?'

'Er – what about the essay?'

'Oh, we'll have plenty of time to do that after dinner.'

'What time's dinner?'

'Seven.'

'That's an hour away. Why don't we just start it now?'

'Oh, I don't feel like it,' she says, pulling out a drawer

and sorting through her collection of nail varnishes. 'What do you think of this colour?' She holds up a pink shade with a purple shimmer.

'It's nice.'

'Marianne bought one as well. I told her we'd have to arrange who could wear it in which week so we didn't end up having "hers and hers" nails!'

'Right,' I say with a weak grin. That must have been on one of their many shopping trips. The shopping trips I wasn't invited on.

'You'll have to do my right hand because I'm crap at painting with my left,' says Lizzie, and holds it out.

I paint her nails, slowly, carefully.

'What do you think we should do for my birthday?' says Lizzie suddenly.

'It's not for another two months.'

'I know. I was thinking about a theme park.'

'There isn't one round here.'

'What about Alton Towers?'

'That's miles away!'

'It's only a couple of hours.'

'How would we get there?'

Lizzie stares. 'Our parents would drive us, of course. Yours and mine. I'd invite Yasmine, Maia and Marianne, so we'd probably need two cars.'

I try to imagine what my parents will say if I ask them to drive us on a four-hour round trip so we can go to Alton Towers. 'Uh, I don't think my parents will like that idea much.'

Lizzie takes the nail-varnish bottle from me and sighs

impatiently. 'Oh, stop being so gloomy, Em. The least you could do is ask them.'

'What if they say no?' Which they will.

'Then we ask someone else, duh.'

'Oh, OK.'

'God, Em, you always over-react.' She paints her left hand sulkily.

I feel terrible. She's right, I do always over-react. Why do I take everything so seriously?

I cast about in my mind for something I can say to relieve the awkward silence. 'How's Adam?'

'Dumped him.'

'Oh. When?'

'Yesterday.'

I can't believe she didn't mention it today at school. There was a time when she would have been straight on the phone to me about something like that. I can't think of anything else to say, except: 'Why?'

She shrugs, finishes her nails and spreads them out to admire them. 'He was just getting so boring. And all he wanted to talk about was when we were going to have sex.' She rolls her eyes. 'And he had bad breath.'

'Bad breath?'

'Yeah.' She grins suddenly. 'I used to have to hold my breath while I was kissing him so I couldn't smell it.'

I giggle. 'You never told me.'

'I don't tell you *everything*.' She bats her eyelashes at me. We are friends again. I feel relief wash over me. It's so strong it makes my hands tremble. Or is that because I'm hungry?

Dinner is uncomfortable. Lizzie's parents are being icily polite to each other. 'Please would you pass the salt?' 'Certainly.' Etc.

'Wish Sam was still here,' Lizzie mutters to me. 'At least he was a laugh.'

Sam is her elder brother. He's at university, studying bio-engineering, whatever that is. He's really clever. Lizzie's always moaning that he got the clever genes while she got the stupid ones.

I try to eat as fast as possible. It is dawning on me that we haven't started Lizzie's assignment, and we are no nearer to doing so. It is a quarter to eight when we go back upstairs. We have an hour and three quarters before my mum picks me up.

'Right.' I hit her on the shoulder with Jane Austen's *Emma*. 'No more procrastinating. You have to do this now.'

'No more whatting?'

Inwardly I kick myself. 'Procrastinating. It means not doing what you're supposed to be doing.'

'You see, Em, this is why you should be writing the essay, not me.'

'I am *not* doing it for you,' I say firmly. 'And if you don't start writing it now I'll just go home.'

Lizzie groans, but she does pick up a pen and a writing pad. I explain the story as concisely as I can.

'Sounds really dull,' says Lizzie.

'No, it's OK actually. Better than that awful Laurie Lee stuff we had to do back in Year Eight. And at least this heroine isn't perfect. She's really bitchy.'

'So what have I got to write?' asks Lizzie, scratching off a bit of nail varnish from the side of her finger. I show her the list of essay titles. Her face drops. 'I can't write any of those. I wouldn't even know where to start.'

'Yes, you can. I'll help you. Look, start with this . . .'

We work solidly for the next hour and a half, but only because I keep nagging Lizzie. She is the worst person I know for finding other things to do. She looked out of the window and tried to get me to count the number of sparrows in the tree. She said she needed to go to the toilet. She asked me if I was thirsty. She grumbled that the nail varnish wasn't as nice as she'd thought.

By the time my mum comes to pick me up, I am exhausted. But the essay is nearly finished, and Lizzie assures me she can do the rest on her own.

'Thanks, Emily,' she says, giving me a huge hug. 'What would I do without you? You're the best friend in the world.'

I feel ashamed for my nasty thoughts about her.

we just want you to do your best

When I get home, Mum makes me have a bath. 'All that work,' she says. 'You need winding down.'

All that work – yeah, right. And none of it mine. While I was at Lizzie's I had pushed away the niggling thought of my homework. Now I'm home and I still haven't done any of it. Three subjects due in tomorrow.

For a moment, I consider telling Mum about the massive pile of stuff I haven't done yet. I try an angle I know she'll be worried about. 'Mum,' I say as she runs the bath for me. 'I'm a bit worried about the exams.'

'Oh Emily.' She comes and gives me a hug with slippery hands. 'You've got lots of time before then; just keep working and you'll be fine.'

'But there's so much to do,' I say.

She takes hold of my shoulders and looks me in the face. 'We just want you to do your best,' she says firmly. 'No one can ask for more than that. As long as you work hard, you'll do yourself justice. At the end of the day, they're just exams. Everyone hates exams. I hated them too, but you just have to grit your teeth and get through them. And I bet by the time they're over, you'll be wondering what all the fuss was about, hmm?'

I smile weakly. She doesn't have the faintest idea.

I rush my bath. No point luxuriating in the bubbly water, there's work to be done. By five past ten I'm back in my room and in my pyjamas. I'm half-way through the Maths. Still got to do the Science worksheet and finish the comprehension exercise for English – better make a start.

Mum and Dad come up to bed. Mum sticks her head round the door and frowns. 'Why are you still up?'

'I've just got to finish off a bit of homework,' I say. 'I didn't quite get it all done at Lizzie's.'

'Hmm.' She's not happy about it. 'Well, no later than eleven, all right? You can't possibly concentrate at school if you're too tired.'

'OK,' I say, forcing my face into a cheerful expression.

I finish the Maths and pick up the English comprehension. I can hear Mum and Dad murmuring to each other as they get into bed. The springs creak. Mum yawns. I can feel myself yawning in sympathy, but I've got a lot to do before I can go to sleep. I am careful not to make any noise. The walls in this house are too thin.

My brain seems to have tuned into Work FM. I stare at the page, forcing myself to concentrate. Read the question, process the instruction, put pen to paper, write the answer. Read the question, process the instruction, put pen to paper, write the answer . . .

Finish the English, start the Science. Here I run into a brick wall. I simply do not understand what the worksheet wants me to do. The instructions seem to contradict each other, and the diagram doesn't relate to the question at all.

No, I am being stupid. It must be me. I'm not reading it properly. I read it six times. I am no nearer to understanding what I have to do.

I screw up my eyes in despair and slap my hand against my head, forgetting the noise it makes. The sound is unexpectedly loud. Have they heard me? I look at my clock. Twenty to twelve. My whole body freezes as my ears strain for any noise in the next room. The bedsprings creak, and for a moment I forget to breathe. Then there is a snuffling noise and Dad starts to snore.

I feel dizzy with relief, and I pick up the Science sheet again. Right, you stupid girl, just *read it*. It can't be that hard, you are an intelligent girl.

I read it again. Again it makes no sense. My eyes burn, but I will not cry. This is just a silly setback. I will have to go in tomorrow and tell Mr Joannou that I do not understand the homework. That is what any normal person would do.

But the thought of admitting to the teacher, in front of the class, that I could not understand a simple worksheet fills me with chilling dread. I have seen the way Mr Joannou tears pupils to pieces before. He can be so scathing about people who haven't done their homework. The humiliation would stay with me for weeks. Everyone would laugh. Wild thoughts dash through my head. Perhaps I could skip Science? Fall over on purpose and have to go to Medical for the lesson? Fake an asthma attack? But I don't have asthma, so that wouldn't work. Maybe I could develop it suddenly? I've heard you can get it later in life.

No, no, no! I go to hit myself on the head again, but remember just in time that it's too loud. I look around desperately. Punch a pillow? Too loud again. I settle for pinching the skin on my upper thigh. Hard. Really hard.

Ouch. That really hurts. Good.

Better now. I reach for the Science sheet again and hold it in front of my eyes, forcing myself to read it over and over.

It is half past twelve when I allow myself to go to bed.

'Thanks so much for last night,' Lizzie says when she sees me. 'You saved my life.'

I smile. 'That's OK. Just don't forget to hand it in.'

'Where's yours?'

'Handed it in last week.' I yawn suddenly.

'And what time did *you* go to bed last night?' asks Lizzie slyly. 'Watching late-night TV?'

'Yeah,' I say, stifling another yawn. There's no point explaining.

'I hope Mr Joannou doesn't want our worksheets,' comments Lizzie as we make our way to registration. 'I didn't even bother to look at it.'

'Didn't you?'

'Nah. I have much better things to do with my time. Like wash my hair.' She laughs. 'What was it like?'

'Er.' I cannot possibly say I couldn't do it. She

21

wouldn't believe me anyway, and if by any remote chance she did believe me, Lizzie would think that was the most hilarious piece of news in the world. I can just hear her in my head. '*You* couldn't do it? Well, that must be a first! Wait, let me write this down, quick! We must record this auspicious day. The Day Emily Couldn't Do Her Homework!' Although, of course, she wouldn't say 'auspicious'.

'Well? Hello?' Lizzie waves her hand in front of my face. 'Earth to Planet Emily? What's the Science work-sheet like?'

'Sorry.' I force a smile. 'Miles away. It was all right, I guess.'

She nods, losing interest. A small hard knot forms in my stomach region. I know it's there, I can practically put my fingers on it. I know what it is. It's the Science homework. I've had this before. When I am dreading something, it doesn't matter how much I tell myself to calm down, my body reacts in its own way. When I was little, Mum used to say that panic was all in my mind. Being nervous wouldn't help me get through it. So I squashed everything into this knot. It's my way of dealing with worry. Science isn't until this afternoon, but that will just give the lump time to get bigger. It will stop me concentrating in other lessons. And it will certainly make it impossible for me to eat my lunch.

However, I am a past master of hiding my stomach knot. No one will ever know it is there because I am such a good actress. I can look as though I am paying attention, whereas actually my mind is somewhere completely different. I also have a whole range of avoidance/excuse tactics. When Lizzie says to me at lunchtime, 'Aren't you having any lunch?' I say, 'I ate it all at break.'

'When? I didn't see you.'

'When you went to the toilet. I suddenly got really hungry.'

'Maybe you've got worms,' says Maia, winking at me. 'Our dog gets those.'

'Are you calling Emily a dog?' says Marianne, in mock horror. Everyone laughs, and I laugh too, hiding my suspicion that Marianne would very much like to call me a dog. And many other names too, I'm sure.

But now nobody is interested in whether I have or have not had any lunch. See? I'm *good* at this.

But finally it's Science and I can't hide any more. Mr Joannou is going to be really disappointed in me. I drag my feet on the way to the lesson until Lizzie, of all people, says, 'Oh, hurry *up*, Emily – you don't want detention, do you?'

Yes, Lizzie. I would rather have detention for the next three years than face the humiliation that awaits me on the other side of that door.

We sit down and I take my books out of my bag with shaking hands. I am breathing quickly, shallowly, and sweat is breaking out all over.

'Good afternoon,' says Mr Joannou swiftly. 'Please copy down the date, title and learning objective of today's lesson.' Everyone around me picks up their pens but I cannot. I weigh twenty stone suddenly and am incapable of lifting my arm.

'Now, about the homework,' says Mr Joannou.

This is it. Take me now, ground, swallow me whole.

'I do apologise,' Mr Joannou continues. 'I'm afraid I gave you the wrong two pages. I mean, one of them was the right one, but the other one had got mixed up with my Year Twelves. So you couldn't possibly have done the homework. The diagram was the wrong one. I apologise if any of you wasted time trying to work it out.'

What?

No, this can't be right. Teachers aren't supposed to do this. They can't.

'I thought you said it was OK?' whispers Lizzie.

'Huh? Oh yeah, don't know what I was thinking about,' I gabble uselessly. 'Probably on Planet Emily again, you know.' I twizzle my finger by my temple, indicating that I am certifiably insane.

Which I am. Or Mr Joannou is. How could he *do* this to me? Because of *him* I have not had any lunch and I have no idea what happened in this morning's lessons.

I hate him. He should be sacked for this. He's not supposed to get things wrong – doesn't he realise how much stress I'm under?

No, it's me that's the stupid one. I wasn't even clever enough to realise the sheet was the wrong one. It hadn't even *occurred* to me that Mr Joannou might have made a mistake. I am such an idiot!

Emily, you are crazy. Pull yourself together.

I pick up my pen and begin to write. My stomach, released from the knot, grumbles with hunger.

mega-brain

We get the Lit assignments back the following week. I get 92 per cent – an A. Lizzie gets 71 per cent – a B. She is over the moon.

'Hey, how about that! And I didn't even know what I was talking about! What do you think, Em? I got a B! Isn't that the most hilarious thing ever?'

No. It isn't hilarious and I'll tell you why. It isn't hilarious because you, who spent about two hours writing it the night before (except you didn't really write it because I told you what to write), got a decent grade when actually you should have failed the assignment. And I, who spent a whole week reading the book and three evenings in my holidays writing my essay, *deserved* my mark. How come she's got away with it? And, at the back of my mind, I wonder why I didn't quite make the A★ grade. Only one more mark and it would have been an A★, not an A. I spent hours on that essay. How could I have made it better? Where did I lose 8 per cent?

'Yes,' I say, and paint my smile on. 'It's really good, Liz. Well done.'

'What did you get?' she says, and then laughs. 'As if I need to ask. You did get an A★, didn't you?'

'Not quite. I only got 92 per cent.'

'*Only* 92 per cent? Oh, stop rubbing it in, Em.' She laughs. 'Mega-brain strikes again.'

'Yeah.' I laugh too. 'Mega-brain.' I catch Marianne watching me and for a moment I am afraid. She has seen through my laugh, she knows what I am. She has seen inside to the bundle of mistakes and failures that I hide. She can see that it's all a façade – that my 'natural intelligence' is simple hard work. The 'mega-brain' doesn't exist at all. But then she turns back to Yasmine, and I see that actually she wasn't looking at me at all.

'Are we going out tonight, then?' asks Maia, breaking into my thoughts.

'Yeah!' says Lizzie enthusiastically. 'Destiny has a deal on drinks tonight.'

'Oh, do we have to go there again?' says Maia, pulling a face. 'We always go there.'

'That's because it's the only nightclub that'll let us in,' grins Lizzie. It's not really a nightclub, of course. I mean, not a proper one with loads of twenty-somethings and cocaine. It's a glorified disco that admits kids over fourteen. Although I've seen Year Eights from school in there, so the bouncers can't be that good at keeping the kiddies out. I'm beginning to feel a bit old for it, but ~~ loves it. And I have to confess, they do really nice ~~holic cocktails. Marianne usually sneaks a ~~eers out of her parents' house beforehand so ~~e a proper drink too.

Mum isn't thrilled I'm going out. 'But it's Tuesday,' she says.

'Yes,' I agree.

'It's a school night, Emily. And you had a late one last night again. I really don't think you should go.'

I am a bit tired, but I can't let my friends go without me. Besides, the deal on drinks only runs on Tuesdays, and they play our favourite music that night too. She *knows* we mostly go on Tuesdays. Why's she kicking up a fuss now?

'No,' she says suddenly. 'I'm sorry, Emily, but you can't go.'

'What? Why not?'

'Because,' she says, looking all serious, 'this is your GCSE year. You can go out during the week next year. I really think you need to concentrate on your work at the moment. I mean, you were round at Lizzie's again yesterday.'

'Oh Mum, don't go on at me. I need to spend time with my friends too.'

'Your GCSEs are more important than your friends.'

Now I *know* she's wrong. GCSEs can be re-sat. You don't get a second chance with your friends. But the mess of thoughts in my head means I can't say that clearly. 'No, they're not. You just don't want me to have any fun. Work, work, work! I'm just a test result to you, aren't I?'

'Emily –'

'Don't you think that there are other skills I need apart from academic ones? How am I ever supposed to learn social skills if you never let me go out?'

'Now you're being ridiculous. You know as well as I do how important education is. Your father and I never had the opportunities you have.'

Oh, here we go. The old 'we never got the chance so you have to do it all' speech. I sigh.

'Don't roll your eyes at me, young lady,' snaps Mum. 'I don't care if you like it or not. You're staying in and that's final.'

'All right, all right!' I hold up my hands. 'I get the message. Loud and clear. As always. I'll go and do my homework now.' I stomp out.

'And don't try to get round me by asking your dad, either!' she yells after me.

Lizzie is appalled when I call her up. 'What? They said you couldn't come? Why not?'

'They reckon I should be concentrating on my *GCSEs*.'

Lizzie makes gagging noises at the other end of the phone. 'I swear, if I have to hear that word one more time . . .'

'Tell me about it. Oh Liz, I really want to come.'

'Em, it's cool. Really. We probably won't have that good a time anyway. You know, Maia'll get drunk, like she usually does. Yasmine will flirt with every boy over the age of ten –'

'That's harsh. Twelve at least.'

'And I'll end up sitting in a corner not talking to any-one. You know how it is.'

She's making me smile, even though I know it's not

true. 'Will you tell me all about it tomorrow?'

'Course I will. We'll bring you back a souvenir, OK? Something really bizarre.'

'A pair of boxers?' I suggest. We shriek with laughter.

'Deal,' she says. 'I'll make Yasmine get them for you.'

'Good,' I say, and suddenly I do feel a bit better.

'Don't worry, Emmy, we're bound to be going again soon.'

Emmy. She hasn't called me that since Year Seven. Suddenly I feel eleven again. 'All right. Have a good time.'

'Without you? Never.'

She hangs up. I go to my room, coldly avoiding Mum as she comes out of the lounge.

I start my homework, as I have nothing better to do. Well, I *mean* to start it, but *actually* I start playing with a puzzle my dad gave me years ago. I'd forgotten that it was still on my shelf, but I'm deliberately looking for something to distract me. Mum can make me stay at home, but she can't make me work. Why should I do my homework just because she says so? I'll do it when I'm ready.

It takes me half an hour to figure out the puzzle, as I've completely forgotten how to do it. Then Anthony comes in.

'Hi.'

'Hi.' He's standing in the doorway. 'You OK?'

He shrugs. 'Yeah.' He's lying. I can tell because I'm really good at it myself. I pat the bed next to me. 'Come and sit down.'

He walks in, dragging his feet, and sighs.

'What's the matter?'

'I hate school.'

'Me too.'

'Why do you hate it?'

'Too much work,' I say. 'Too many people nagging me about it.'

He sighs. 'Me too.'

'Too much work?' I ask. 'Already? You're only in Year Seven; there can't be that much.'

'Yes, there is. There's loads. More than I used to get.'

'Sorry, that's secondary school for you.'

'It's all really hard too.'

I frown. 'It shouldn't be that hard.'

'It is! It takes me ages!'

'You should complain. If it's taking you that long.'

He chews his bottom lip and shrugs.

'What?'

He shrugs again. 'It doesn't take everyone else that long.'

'Why not?'

'They're all cleverer than me.'

I laugh without thinking. He stands up, his face flushing pink. 'I knew you wouldn't understand.'

I reach for his arm as he turns to go. 'Wouldn't understand what? Sorry I laughed. I just thought you were being silly.'

'Yeah, that's what everyone thinks! Silly, stupid Anthony! Put him in the front row, 'cos he's too stupid!'

'Whoa, whoa there! Who's calling you stupid?'

'Everyone.' He waves his arms in the air, gesturing lots of people. 'The teachers, the kids . . . everyone. Even the receptionist thinks I'm stupid. She got cross with me because I couldn't remember our telephone number.'

'She's got our phone number in your file.'

'She said she'd lost it.'

'Then she's the stupid one, not you.' I pull on his arm so that he sits down again. 'Don't worry about it.' It seems a really lame thing to say, but I can't think of anything else. 'Sometimes people are just nasty to people they don't know. It'll be OK. It's only been a week or so.'

'Ten days.'

He's counting the days? I put my arm around him. 'It's always hard, starting a new school and having to make new friends.' Now I sound like Mum. 'And the work is a lot harder than primary.'

'And I have six lessons a day.'

'And they're all different subjects, with different teachers.'

'And they all shout at me.'

'I'm sure they don't *all* shout at you.'

He shrugs. 'All right. My ICT teacher doesn't shout at me.'

'There you are, then.'

'But that's because he can't remember my name.'

I grin. 'Maybe that's a good thing, then?'

He lets out a little giggle. 'Yeah.' He sighs and gets up. 'I better go and do my homework.'

'Me too.'

'Emily . . .?'

'Yeah?'

'Are people ever nasty to *you*?'

'What sort of people? Teachers?'

'No, people your own age.'

'Sometimes,' I say. 'Not so much now, though. They were a few years ago, but I think they grew out of it. That's what Mum said anyway.'

'Emily . . .?'

'Yeah?'

'How long before I'm grown up?'

When he's gone I sit and think. Anthony's never done very well at school. He used to get different work from some of the other kids. And there was a really cool teaching assistant at his old school. Maybe she helped him more than we realised. I don't suppose there's an assistant in his new class. There's hardly ever one in my classes. So he's having to do it all himself. No wonder he's finding it hard going. But it's even worse if people are calling him stupid.

He's not stupid, of course. He's just not very good at school stuff. Which is hard luck when you spend thirty hours a week there. I work out the percentage on my calculator, just because I'm curious: 168 hours in a week, so . . . 17.9 per cent if you round it up. Nearly 20 per cent of your childhood years spent at school. What a waste.

It strikes me as really ironic that Anthony is surrounded by people telling him he's stupid, whilst I'm surrounded by people telling me I'm clever.

If I were clever I would have got that extra mark in

my Lit assignment and reached an A★.

The evening lasts several days – at least, that's what it feels like. I haven't even started my homework by the time we sit down to dinner 'as a family'. I am still not speaking to Mum. The girls are all at Destiny by now, having a fantastic time no doubt. Mum just doesn't understand how important my friends are to me. You have to work at being friends. If you don't make an effort, your friends will stop liking you. I read it in a magazine.

'How was school?' asks Dad.

'Horrible,' says Anthony.

'Foul,' I say.

'How nice,' Dad grins. 'My day was pretty revolting too. How about yours, Frances?'

Mum shrugs. 'It was all right, I guess.'

Mum never plays the game.

'Ask Emily what she got for her English essay,' says Anthony suddenly. I turn to him accusingly. 'I saw it on your bed,' he hastily admits.

'Well, Emily?' asks Dad. 'What did you get?'

'Ninety-two per cent,' I mumble, poking my cauliflower cheese with the fork.

'That's excellent,' says Dad. 'Well done.'

'Very good,' says Mum. She smiles at me. 'What grade is that?'

'A.'

'Fantastic.' She winks at me. 'So how come it wasn't an A★?'

I *knew* she was going to say that, I just *knew* it.

'Oh, for God's sake!' I scowl. 'Isn't anything good enough for you?'

Her face falls. 'It was a joke.'

'Emily –' Dad tries to defend her. 'Your mum didn't mean anything by it. It's just that you always get such good marks. Which is great,' he adds hastily, as he can see I'm boiling over. 'And we're so pleased that you're doing so well at school, particularly this year and everything . . .'

'Go on!' I shout suddenly, making everyone jump. 'Say it! Just say it! Say it's my GCSE year! Because I might have forgotten, you know! Because nobody reminds me more than every thirty minutes – and my memory retention isn't that good, you know!' I stand up sharply, knocking my drink over. 'I've had enough.'

When I get to my room I throw myself on my bed and wait to cry. But nothing happens. Instead a heavy, dark, tired feeling comes over me, like a black cloud in my heart. It is squeezing emotions and thoughts out of me. It is smothering my mind, my body, my soul. Soon it will engulf me totally and I will sink into the abyss. Noises, voices and memories whirl through my head. I hear the stupid things I've said; see the face Mum uses when she is disappointed in me; replay the awkward moments with Lizzie. Piles of work drift through my mind, along with insistent voices of teachers. I try to block them out, but they are too loud, too insistent.

I can hear Lizzie saying, 'Oh wait, you must hear the really bad joke Emily told me the other day – poor thing, she thought it was funny!'

Mr Joannou's voice: 'I'm very sorry, I'm afraid I gave you the wrong two pages. So you couldn't possibly have done the homework.'

Marianne's sneering tone: 'Are you calling Emily a dog?'

Mum: 'So how come it wasn't an A$\star$?'

Dad: 'It's just that you always get such good marks.'

Anthony: 'They all shout at me.'

All those voices, going round and round in my head. Round and round in the swirling cloud, making my eyes burn because they are so dry. I want to cry, it would make me feel better.

Or would it? Won't crying actually make me feel worse? After all, there's nothing really to cry about. I'm a bit overworked; I'm feeling left out by my friends. Mum would say that's no reason to cry. Everyone goes through times when they feel overwhelmed. The trick is to grit your teeth and get through it. Crying won't change anything.

I lie there, staring and staring into the dark. I feel like such a fake. They all think I'm good at stuff – clever, a good memory – but I can't tell them they're under an illusion. None of this is real. I am not really the me they think they know – I'm someone else. Someone not as nice. Definitely someone not as clever. I've just been lucky so far. Nobody has realised that I've been playing a part. But I can't tell them. I don't even have the words. And it would disappoint them all so much. Especially Mum.

I see her face fall again, over and over in my mind.

She really didn't mean it seriously. Why couldn't I laugh it off? She didn't deserve my response. I was horrible to her, horrible. I am an ungrateful daughter. She has given me everything – and this is how I repay her?

Dad knocks. I don't reply, but he comes in anyway. 'Emily,' he says, without waiting for me to say anything, 'I realise you're a bit stressed at the moment, but you must try not to take it out on us. Your mum's really upset by what you said to her, and she thinks it's all her fault. She doesn't understand why you should be angry with her.'

I sit up. 'I'm not angry with her.'

'Aren't you? What about this evening? Weren't you going out?'

'Oh yeah.' Funny, that seems like hours ago. 'But I wasn't really angry with her about that. I mean, I was earlier . . .' I trail off. He doesn't understand – how could he? *I* don't understand.

He sighs. 'Just try to remember you're not the only one in this family,' he says, and goes.

You're not the only one in this family. No one knows that better than I do. The other members of my family press down on me constantly. I am always aware of where they are, how they feel, what they think of me. Everything I do is reflected in their eyes. Even Anthony has opinions of me. He thinks I am someone to turn to. Someone who can help him out. But who can help me out? I have to be strong, for everyone else. I have to be strong.

why are you putting
yourself down?

Lizzie barely looks at me the next morning. I try to catch her eye during Eng Lang, but she's talking to Marianne. Is she blanking me on purpose? I don't have a chance to talk to her before I go to double Art, and only Maia takes Art with me.

I love Art. It's the best thing in the world. It's the only thing that takes me away from myself, from the failures and the disappointments and the pressure.

I am drawing a still life of velvet curtains, lace and a violin. I love the colours: the deep, rich red of the velvet, the creamy white of the lace and the ruddy brown shiny streaks of the violin. The light reflects off the body of the violin, making strange and unidentifiable shapes in its contours.

I can lose myself in my drawings. Hours can pass without meaning, and all thoughts recede into insignificance. There is only the picture. And my hand, manipulating the brush or pencil or pen as surely, and with as much familiarity, as I brush my teeth in the morning. I know what works and what doesn't. The painting cannot argue back, cannot express its opinion of me. It cannot put pressure on me. I love the painting.

When I am drawing, I can convince myself that I am a good person; that I am worth something.

It doesn't last, but that is because other people intrude.

'Emily,' says Mrs Knowles, standing over my shoulder. 'That's beautiful. You've really got the curve of the violin there, and I love the way you've shaded the velvet. It looks almost real.'

'Yes,' I say, 'but I still can't get the lace right.'

'The lace is fine, Emily. There's nothing wrong with it. It's a lovely piece of work.'

'Oh,' I say unhappily. 'It's not finished yet. And I got the perspective wrong in the top right-hand corner.'

Mrs Knowles puts a hand on my shoulder. 'Why are you putting yourself down? Surely even you can see it's an excellent drawing, particularly for someone of your age. Well done.' She pats me on the shoulder and misery returns.

Excellent for someone of my age. That means it's rubbish. No fifteen-year-old can draw well, not compared with real artists. She's trying to console me.

But a small part of me whispers, 'She's right. It is good. Look at Katie's picture. It's nowhere near as good as yours. And Stephanie's is a good drawing, but she's spoilt it with the shading. The lines are all higgledy-piggledy. Yours is better than theirs, you know it is.'

'Yes,' argues the other, bigger part of me, 'but you shouldn't be comparing yourself with them. You have

38

your own standards and you know what's good and what isn't. And your picture is OK, but it's not as good as you could do if you put your mind to it. You're just not trying hard enough. *You're not doing your best.*'

When Maia comes past she stops and says, 'Oh Emily, that's brilliant.'

I force a smile. 'No, it's not really. I think I could have done it better.'

'Really?' She looks impressed. 'I couldn't have done that. You have *got* to be an artist when you leave school.'

I don't have to reply because she has moved on, but I feel a tiny warm patch somewhere in the region of my belly button. Could I be an artist? Visions of my paintings hung in a gallery rise before me: exhibitions, champagne, sitting by the sea with my easel and paint palette. I could live in an apartment decorated just the way I liked. I could attend parties and openings and talk knowledgeably about Picasso and Monet. Perhaps I could even win a prize . . .

I shake my head angrily. What are you thinking about, idiot? You couldn't possibly be an artist. You're not good enough. Who on earth would *pay* for one of your scrawls? I bite my lip hard, furious for allowing myself to get carried away in an impossible dream. The more I look at my picture now, the more I hate it. I want to rip it up and throw it away, but I can't because it's part of my GCSE coursework. But I *can* put it in a folder and never look at it again.

When Art is over, I am in a bad mood. I go to meet the others for lunch, but they are not in the usual place.

I go to the form room and they are there, clustered in a little group. Yasmine is in the middle.

'So he called me, right, just before midnight. I mean, can you *imagine*! My parents went spare. And my dad gave him a right earful. I don't suppose he'll call back,' she ends dolefully.

'But he was gorgeous,' says Marianne. 'I fancied him too, but I didn't have the guts to talk to him.'

'How old did he say he was?' asks Maia, eyes alight.

'Nineteen,' says Yasmine. 'He said he was studying Biology at uni.'

'Biology, eh?' says Lizzie and raises her eyebrows suggestively. Laughter erupts. I drag my feet towards them. It feels as though I am intruding, but that's ridiculous. These are my friends!

'Hi,' I say, smiling. 'What's going on?'

'Oh, just some bloke Yasmine met last night,' says Marianne dismissively. 'Shall we go to lunch?'

The others nod, and we turn to go. I gulp slightly. They haven't told me anything about last night. I wasn't there – I don't belong. Until we all do something else together, I can't be part of the group. At least that's what it feels like.

I make one last-ditch attempt. I fall in beside Yasmine as we head down the stairs. 'What happened, then?'

'Oh, not much,' she says. 'We saw him at the bar and Lizzie dared me to go and speak to him. I felt really embarrassed.' I doubt it. Yasmine is the most outgoing of all of us. She does things that would make me cringe inside. 'Anyway, he bought me a drink and then he asked for my phone number.'

'Bet you wish now you hadn't given it to him!' I laugh.

'No, why should I?' She throws me a puzzled look.

'Because of waking up your parents, and your dad shouting and everything.'

She shrugs. 'I don't care. It's not my fault he rang so late. Hey, wait up!' She puts on a burst of speed to catch up with Maia.

I walk along behind, feeling like I just messed up again but I don't know how.

'Hey,' says Lizzie. Maybe I have another chance to rejoin the group.

'Hey,' I respond, grinning. 'Did you get me those boxers, then?'

Lizzie looks bemused. 'What boxers?'

'The ones from a boy at the club. You said you'd get Yasmine to get them.'

'Oh Emily,' she says, smiling, 'you didn't think I was *serious*, did you?'

Then she goes to talk to Marianne.

honey

In the last lesson, Lizzie whispers to me, 'Corner shop. After school.'

The corner shop is just outside the school gates. Whenever anything is planned, it usually starts there. I wonder if it's a fight. The boys' grammar is always having fights with the private boys' school two streets away. It reminds me that I'm glad to go to an all-girls school.

But as it turns out, it's not a fight. Instead, we are meeting up with Marianne's sister, who is in Year Twelve. Hélène is only eleven months older than Marianne, but she acts like she's twenty. I feel young around her. People suddenly age when they reach the Sixth. From uniformed girls with blazers and backpacks to cool and trendy young women who have piercings and are allowed to wear make-up.

'Hi girls,' says Hélène, taking a drag of her cigarette. 'Marianne thought I should let you in on a gig in town.'

'Gig?' asks Lizzie, her eyes lighting up just like Hélène's cigarette. 'What sort of gig?'

'The boys' Sixth are putting on a show. To raise

money for charity,' says Hélène. 'It's at the Tavern on Saturday. I'm gonna be on the door and I can get you lot in if you like. It's for over-sixteens, but once you're in they don't usually ask for ID at the bar. You know what the Tavern's like. Besides, half the Sixth aren't eighteen yet and they're always in there buying drinks.' Including you, I think. I don't bother to mention the fact that half of us aren't even sixteen yet, let alone legally old enough for alcohol.

There is a chorus of 'Wow!' 'Cool!' and various other noises of approval.

'Excellent!' says Lizzie, her eyes shining. I nod enthusiastically, although this sort of adventure makes me nervous. I know the Tavern has a reputation for trouble, and the thought of mixing with so many older people gives me butterflies.

'I'll see you on Saturday, then?' says Hélène, giving us a superior I'm-happy-to-do-you-a-favour nod. 'Nine-thirty. Don't be late.'

'What time does it finish?' I blurt.

Hélène looks at me with a slight curl to her lip. 'Whenever the night is over, honey.' She walks away, making me feel about two centimetres tall.

Of course, Marianne is the centre of attention after this. 'You're so lucky to have an older sister,' says Maia enviously. 'She's so cool.'

'She's not like that at home.' Marianne shakes her head, enjoying it. 'She's so messy. And she leaves Tampax boxes all over the place. It drives my stepdad crazy. *And* she borrows my clothes.'

'Is everyone up for it, then?' asks Lizzie, looking around.

'Definitely,' says Maia.

'Just try to keep me away,' grins Yasmine.

'Emily?'

I force my face into an expression of enthusiasm. 'Of course. Count me in.'

Marianne looks at me carefully, and then nods.

What does that mean?

Of course I have no intention of telling my parents where I'm going. There's no way they'd let me set foot in the Tavern, so I say I'm going to Destiny again. Mum pulls a face.

'Saturday night's not a good night to be in town, Emily.' But then she sees my stony glare and she remembers that she didn't let me go out last night. 'Oh, all right.' She tries to look happy about it but I can tell she's faking. 'We'll come and pick you up from there – half eleven?'

'No, it's all right,' I say hastily. 'I'll get the bus home.'

'You most certainly will not. Not on a Saturday night. Your father will pick you up.'

'All right, but can we make it twelve?' I try.

She tuts, but then nods. 'Seeing as it's not a school night.'

'And can he pick me up from the newsagent's? You know parking is impossible at Destiny.'

Which it is.

'Oh, all right. But I hope you're not going to sleep in

all day on Sunday. And don't put your drink down, even for a moment. And don't go anywhere on your own.'

'I'll make sure a nice boy keeps me company.'

'Don't joke about this, Emily. You must keep yourself safe.'

I know what's brought this on. She watched a programme the other night about date-rape drugs. I promise faithfully not to do anything that will allow me to have any fun. If she knew where I was really going she'd blow her top.

if you're sure

I can't do any homework on Saturday. I am only too aware of the importance of the evening. I spend the whole day worrying. Worrying about what to wear, what to say, what to do when people talk to me, what to do if people *don't* talk to me, what to drink, how to behave . . . the list is endless.

I do start my homework with all good intentions, but somehow whenever I look at a book or a sheet, my mind starts buzzing about this evening. By lunchtime I still haven't done anything, but it's important to keep up appearances. I spread out my homework on my desk and pick up a pen so that I can start to write whenever Mum pops in. She cannot leave me alone. She is constantly checking up on me. The longest I go without her nosying in is half an hour. In the end I shut my door, but that doesn't stop her.

Knock, knock. 'Would you like a cup of tea, Emily?'

'No thanks.'

Knock, knock. 'I'm just popping to the shop. Is there anything you need?'

'No thanks.'

Knock, knock. 'Emily, Anthony says he can't find his ruler. You haven't got it, have you?'

'No.'

At lunchtime she comes in to see how much I've done. Well, that's not what she says, but I know it's the truth. I show her last week's homework and she says, 'Goodness, haven't you done a lot? Well done. Looks like you deserve a nice long lunch break – at least an hour.'

Woo-hoo.

The afternoon isn't much better. I tell Mum I need to do some research on the internet, so she lets me use the computer in the spare room. We only have one computer in our house. Mum says we don't need more than one, even though I've told her I need a computer in my room. I spend most of the afternoon playing games. I have a Shakespeare site open in another window, so I can flick between them if someone comes in. I also paint my nails, mess them up by mistake and have to do them all over again.

Before I know it, it's seven o'clock. I hardly eat anything for dinner but Mum doesn't really notice. She's too busy trying to get Anthony to talk about school again. She hasn't realised that the more she asks, the less he'll tell her.

I have a shower and wash my hair. I still don't know what to wear. I've only been in the Tavern once before and that was during the day. Should I wear jeans or a skirt? How short? I also have to bear in mind that Mum

47

thinks I'm going to Destiny, so I have to wear something suitable for that.

I finally settle for a short skirt, knee-high boots and a
tight black top. I make up my face carefully – Lizzie
gave me her old sparkly eyeliner and I'm still trying to
get the hang of it.

When I'm finished I hardly recognise the person in
the mirror. She looks grown-up. It's not me. But then,
do I want to be me anyway? Maybe this Emily is more
confident, more sure of herself. She certainly looks it.

I go down, feeling happier and more excited than I
have for a long time.

'You look nice,' says Dad.

Mum looks me up and down. 'Are you sure you want
to wear something that short?'

'Yes,' I say, meeting her eyes. She shrugs.

'All right, then, if you're sure.'

Immediately, I am *not* sure. Is it too short? Does it
make my legs look fat? Am I asking for it because I'm
wearing a short skirt? What if everyone else is in jeans?
There must be something wrong with it if Mum
doesn't like it. But she hasn't *said* she doesn't like it.
What does she really think?

How the hell does she do this to me? With one innocent
question, she makes me doubt all my judgements. I *hate*
that she can do this to me. It's like pulling away the floor
from under me. My decisions suddenly have no basis:
why did I decide to wear this, how did I think I was
going to get away with that? *Aargh!*

Dad notices that my face darkens, and he jumps up.

'I'll drop you off.'

'No, Dad, it's OK. I'll get the bus.'

He's already pulling on his jacket. 'No, it's fine, Emily. I'd rather drop you off and make sure you meet up with your friends all right.'

My life is one long battle. I give in on this one. But what am I supposed to do at the other end? Why do my parents make everything so difficult for me? Now Dad's forced me to lie to him.

'Where are they?' he asks, just as I knew he would, outside Destiny.

I look at my watch. 'Oh, they're probably inside by now. I'm a bit late.'

'All right,' he says. 'But you go straight in, mind. I don't want you hanging around the town.'

'*Yes*, Dad,' I groan, but somehow it's not so annoying when he says it. If Mum had said that to me, I'd have jumped down her throat. She just has a way of saying things that makes you think she has a hidden agenda. Dad doesn't have any agenda, he's transparent as glass. He grins at me.

'Have a good time, then. Try not to bewitch too many boys.' He winks.

'See you later,' I say, getting out.

'Twelve on the dot at the newsagent's,' he says, before the door slams and he drives off. I wave at him until he's rounded the corner and then I set off to the Tavern.

It's not far, just a ten-minute walk, but the night is chilly and I didn't bring a coat. It's threatening to rain too, and I just hope it holds off until I get there.

49

I walk with my head down, trying not to catch anyone's eye. There are groups of people heading in different directions, including a large group of boys, who whistle at me and make suggestive comments. I walk past as quickly as I can, wishing I wasn't on my own.

'There she is!' Lizzie waves at me. 'We were just about to go in.'

I do a quick appraisal of what everyone else is wearing. Yasmine looks absolutely stunning as usual, in laced-up jeans and a halter-neck top. Marianne's looking OK, but I'm pleased to see she's botched her mascara and has lipstick on her teeth. Maia and Lizzie are wearing similar outfits to mine. I breathe a sigh of relief. I have passed Test One.

Hélène grins at us as we approach the door. 'Hi, girls. Fiver and ID please.'

We hold out our money and Hélène says, 'Fine. In you go.' Not one of us has shown her any ID.

The Tavern is baking hot already. The tall stools are taken, so we find a space against a wall and stand awkwardly, looking around. 'We should get drinks,' I say.

'Good idea,' says Lizzie. 'Why don't you go and get the first round?'

'Er.' I am stumped. I only have twenty pounds in my purse. There are five of us. It will pretty much clean me out, I should think.

'Yeah, that's a good idea,' says Marianne. 'We can take turns to get the rounds in. Saves us all going up to the bar at the same time.'

I have no choice, although I suspect we may not get

five rounds in. In which case, some lucky person will be getting free drinks all night. What's the betting it's Marianne?

I squeeze my way to the bar, desperately trying to remember the orders. I am also terrified that the barman will be able to tell I am under age and won't serve me.

But in the end, he barely glances at me. He listens intently, asking me to speak up, then dashes around pulling pints, opening fridges and mixing spirits. The top of the bar is swimming in beer and I put my arm in it by mistake.

I am wondering how on earth I am supposed to carry all five glasses/bottles when Maia appears at my elbow. 'Hey, well done,' she says. 'I'll take these if you can grab the rest.'

'Thanks.'

The atmosphere is definitely hotting up, and some guy has started to test the microphones on a makeshift stage. There's an electric keyboard and a guitar, as well as a set of drums. It is all really cramped and I wonder how the performers are going to move around.

'What do you think of the local totty, then?' asks Yasmine, looking around.

I have to say I am quite impressed. There are a lot of sixth-formers from both the boys' grammar and the girls' county. There are some really good-looking blokes around.

We stand for a while, clutching our drinks and sneaking looks at the boys. We are pretending to talk to each other but it's all for show. Marianne laughs too loudly, throwing her hair back, at some joke that she hasn't even heard properly. Lizzie accidentally spills some of her beer down her skirt and has to go to the Ladies to wash it off. Maia anxiously adjusts and readjusts her top, whilst Yasmine simply looks supremely cool, making eye contact with every boy that brushes past her.

And me? I just stand there, feeling as though my legs are too fat and my hands are too big. And my fringe keeps falling in my eyes, just like Miss Collins at school, but I'm not sure whether it's cool to leave it there, so I can peek up through a curtain of hair, or whether I should nonchalantly tuck it behind my ear.

I am thankful when the show starts. The applause is so loud and the catcalls so frequent it's sometimes difficult to hear what's going on, but it's good. It's funny, very funny. There are spoofs of the latest films, and pop songs with the lyrics rewritten. There's a stand-up comedian ('He's *gorgeous,*' says Lizzie in my ear) and a magician who's terrible on purpose and makes me laugh so hard I nearly wet myself.

'This is brilliant!' I shout in Lizzie's ear. She turns and grins back at me, nodding.

'Can't wait till we're in the sixth form!' she shouts back. I feel the same way. Year Eleven is horrible – you're not grown up but you're not kids any more. It's like a sort of limbo: nobody knows what to do with you, and you don't know what to do with yourself either. But in Year Twelve everything changes. You don't have to wear school uniform any more. People treat you with a bit more respect. You're trusted to make decisions. I can't wait!

When the show finishes there's so much applause that it makes my ears hurt. The five of us are stamping our feet and yelling, along with everyone else. The boys come on to take their bows, and the comedian winks at Lizzie. She nearly falls over in delight and I have to take her arm to steady her. We've only had three rounds, but I'm drinking Bacardi Breezers (Lizzie's recommendation) and I'm feeling pretty light-headed.

Then the dancing starts. It's the usual R & B to start with, which is good but hard to dance to. Then some guy puts on the greatest hits of the eighties and we're suddenly all singing along to 'It's Raining Men' and 'I Will Survive' like any cheesy middle-aged club. It's stuff I'd never listen to at home, but somehow when you've got a whole group of people who are really into it, it's instantly the best music in the world.

Yasmine is smooching up close to a stunningly gorgeous boy with floppy blond hair. I vaguely wonder what happened to the boy she met at Destiny on Tuesday. Lizzie manages to find the comedian at some point, and he takes her off to the bar to buy her a drink. Maia, Marianne and I are really getting into it in the small space we have to dance in. Then this boy catches my eye and comes over. He's nice-looking – nothing amazing but friendly and with nice eyes. Before I know it, we're dancing together to 'Summer Nights' from *Grease*, and he's doing all the John Travolta bits and I'm being Olivia Newton-John. Then we swap and he does all the girly bits whilst I try to look as butch as possible. It makes me laugh so much – I can't remember when I last had such a good time.

All too soon I glance at my watch to see it's ten to midnight. 'I have to go,' I yell at the boy. He looks disappointed, and mimes holding a phone to his ear.

'Can I have your phone number?' he mouths.

I am not sure. My mum would kill me if he called in the middle of the night, like Yasmine's bloke did. Besides, I don't really know him, do I? What if he calls and we go out and I decide I don't really like him? Or worse, and far more likely, what if he decides he doesn't like me? Or worse still, what if I give him my number and then he never calls? I'm going to feel really stupid.

I pretend I haven't heard him and wave goodbye. I bump into Lizzie on my way out. She's in a clinch with the comedian. I tap her on the shoulder. 'I have to go,' I yell at her.

'OK,' she nods, and clamps her mouth back over the boy's.

Dad is waiting by the newsagent's when I get there, and I thank God that Destiny and the Tavern are in the same direction so he wouldn't have known which one I was at. 'Had a good time?' he grins, as I get into the car.

'*Yeah,*' I say enthusiastically. My head is still swimming and the noise from the Tavern has made me temporarily deaf. I am also very, very hot, and my black top is sticking to me with sweat.

When we get home, Dad whispers at me, 'Mum's in

bed. I wouldn't make any noise if I were you. You don't want her to know you've had a few.'

I turn to him, eyes wide. He grins. 'What, you think I can't smell the rum?'

I plaster an innocent expression on my face and Dad stifles a laugh. 'Just be thankful it was me picking you up and not her. I don't mind you having a good time as long as you're careful.'

'Night, Dad.' I kiss him on the cheek, something I haven't done for ages. Then I stumble into my room. I can't be bothered to take my make-up off, I'll do it in the morning. I lie on my bed facing the ceiling and wait for the thumping white noise in my head to ease. I grin to myself. What a fantastic evening. Illegal but so much fun! Are the others still there, I wonder? I frown as I think of them all enjoying themselves, partying the night away. I wish I hadn't had to go early. I didn't really mind at the time – well, I didn't really think about it – but now that I'm home, I wish I was still there.

I'm missing out on the gossip again. The others will probably stay on until they're kicked out at – what? Two a.m.? And then they'll straggle out of the club, laughing and stumbling, with their arms around each other. Then they'll get an attack of the munchies and go to the all-night kebab shop. Maybe one of them will throw up, and everyone will cheer.

And I'm not there. *Again*. Why do I always miss out on the best bits? Why are my parents so suffocating? Lizzie's parents don't care what time she gets home. I wish my parents were like that. And Marianne's got an older sister so she can hang out with her.

And I've just realised that Marianne never bought a round. What a surprise. Neither did Yasmine. So I wasted six pounds on them.

And that boy I pulled – I should have given him my phone number, shouldn't I? What if he was really nice and I'm throwing away my only chance to see him again? What if he really liked me and wasn't just being nice? I could have had a boyfriend. My first proper *boyfriend*.

Why am I so stupid?

The euphoria that had accompanied me home is evaporating and instead I start to feel really down. The others are having a fantastic time, and I'm at home, alone. Tears of self-pity well up but I force them back. There's no point in feeling sorry for myself. Instead my sadness turns to anger. It's Mum who's to blame for my not having a good night. She's the one who makes me come home early all the time. Dad would let me stay out all night. He trusts me.

Despair threatens to overwhelm me. I have no life. My friends only tolerate me, they don't really like me. I'm just useful to have around. If I wasn't here they wouldn't really miss me. I am not important, not popular enough. I turn on my side and press my face into the pillow.

raining

It is an effort to wade through my homework the next day. My head hurts from the Bacardi Breezers and I feel heavy. It's raining outside so there's nothing to look at except the raindrops rolling down my window. They are hypnotising.

What is the point in doing all this work? When I finish it, they'll just load me up with another lot. And another, and another. A never-ending cycle of homework. For months and months and months. I bang my hand against my leg in frustration. There is no way out – I am locked into a course and have no way of changing the direction. My *self*, the person who is me, is disappearing into 'GCSE student'. Like the other thousands of GCSE students around the country. We have no identity except the grade on the paper and the number assigned to us. Nobody knows, or cares, who we are. Nobody wants us to have a life. This is not a life; it is an existence.

I finish the work, but I am not really concentrating. For the first time I do not put all my effort into it. Does it matter?

what's the problem?

On Monday, the girls are all yawning and fidgeting their way through the lessons. It appears that Yasmine very nearly had sex with her bloke in some alley somewhere. Until an irate old man opened a window above them and yelled abuse at them. At least, that's the way she tells it.

Marianne didn't manage to pull a single bloke, which makes me secretly pleased, and Maia claims there was no one there she found remotely attractive.

Lizzie's comedian has taken her phone number – 'but he hasn't called yet,' says Lizzie. 'He's probably going to leave it for a few days, just to see if I'm really interested.'

I cannot see the logic in this, but I don't ask her to explain it.

The teachers seem to be in overdrive this week, banging on and on about coursework, homework, class-work and every other kind of work.

When I get my weekend homework back I am astonished to find I have good marks for all of it. I don't understand how this is possible. The marks are pretty much as good as they would have been had I made an effort. So what is going on here? I even find a mistake on my French work, and I point it out to Miss Collins at the end of the lesson.

'A mistake?' she smiles, taking the book from me. 'It's not like me to miss one. Oh yes, you're quite right. Never mind.' She closes the book and hands it back to me. 'You can keep the mark for being so honest.'

I stare at her, but she has started to gather her books and pens. I leave, my head spinning unpleasantly. A mark for being honest? How far is that going to get me in my GCSEs? What does she think she's playing at, not marking our work properly?

I unwisely tell Lizzie, who doesn't care. 'What's the problem, Em?' She is grouchy today. Her parents had a massive row last night and she couldn't get to sleep until three a.m. 'It's just one mark.'

'But one mark could make all the difference between an A and a B.'

'But she's not going to be marking our GCSE paper, is she?'

'No, but she should be preparing us properly, don't you think?'

'Oh, for God's sake,' she snaps suddenly, 'don't you ever think about anything except grades? There are other things in life, you know.'

As half-term approaches, I am ashamed to admit I don't take as much care over my homework as I should. I am swamped with essays, worksheets and test papers. But even when I've done the work, the pile never seems to get any smaller. Why bother? My grades slip slightly but not by much. And nobody has to know. My teachers are far too worried about getting all *their* paperwork done by the various deadlines to worry about my grades.

Around the beginning of October I have a nasty cold and persuade Mum to let me stay home for a day. She's not happy about it. 'But this is a very important year for you, Emily. Are you sure you won't miss too much? Can't you even make it in for half a day?' I shake my head and try to look pathetic.

'I just feel really ill,' I say in an exaggeratedly adenoidal voice. 'And when I stand up I feel dizzy.'

'Well, I'll be in a bit later to check up on you,' she says. 'I've got to go to Anthony's school this morning to talk to his form teacher.'

'Why?'

She frowns. 'I'm not sure. He just said he had a few concerns he'd like to discuss.'

'What sort of concerns?'

'He didn't say.'

'Does Anthony know?'

'No, and you're not to tell him. I don't want him to think I'm poking my nose in.' She pulls the curtains closed. 'Try to get some more sleep. I'll be back at lunchtime for a bit and then I'll have to go into work.'

I nod. Mum works at an estate agent's down the road, so she usually pops home for lunch anyway.

I feel guilty once she's gone. Maybe I should have made the effort to go in today. But the thought of a whole day off without any more homework is too enticing. I spend the day mooching around, playing on the computer and reading. It doesn't go as fast as I had expected, and I find myself getting bored. There's not that much you can do on your own, and it's dull having no one to talk to. Mum pops in as promised at lunchtime (I hear her coming and jump into bed again, faking weakness) and is so gullible that she even agrees to make me lunch in bed. But I then feel guilty about that too. I am perfectly capable of getting my own lunch. I'm just making extra work for her.

'How did the meeting go?' I ask.

An anxious look crosses her face. 'Mr Copley says Anthony isn't doing much homework. And when he is, it looks suspiciously like another student's work.'

'So he's copying?'

She sighs. 'I suppose he must be. I don't know why. Mr Copley said his levels were at the low end but that he should be able to do the work they set. And he says Anthony isn't paying attention in lessons.'

'Oh.'

'I'll have to talk to him. I didn't realise things were this bad – he didn't tell me. But Mr Copley says he's had to give Anthony four lunchtime detentions over the last couple of weeks.'

'What for?'

'Messing around in lessons and not handing in homework. I just don't understand it.'

I take a sip from my cup of soup. 'You do know he doesn't have any extra help now, don't you?'

'Extra help?'

'From a teaching assistant.'

She looks surprised. 'But he shouldn't need any now. He had all that help at King Edward's. They were great at bringing him up to the right level.'

'Yeah, but what if he still needs help?'

'Then why doesn't he ask for it?'

It's my turn to sigh. 'Because he doesn't want anyone to think he's stupid.'

'But he's not stupid.'

'I know that. You know that. But the new school doesn't know that.'

She goes off to work looking puzzled. I feel frustrated that she's so dense. In school, you're on your own. No one looks out for you. Especially if you're in Anthony's position. Moving to a new school is like moving to a new country. It has different rules, different expectations – different people. I'm not at all surprised he's copying homework from other kids. It's a survival technique. I tried it once when I'd forgotten about my Maths homework and I had five minutes to copy it into my book at break. Unfortunately it was Lizzie who lent me her book. I would have done better if I'd just guessed at the answers.

'Put your books away,' says Miss Collins.

I look around. 'What's going on?'

'There's a test today,' says Lizzie.

'What? No one told me!'

'Oh, didn't I mention it?' says Lizzie. 'Sorry, I forgot

to tell you. You weren't in the last lesson.' She shrugs.

She forgot to tell me? About a *test*? How can you forget? I stare at my desk. I think I hear a slight giggle, but I can't be sure. Has she done it on purpose?

I shake my head. I must be going mad, suspecting my best friend of stitching me up. I reach for the blank paper Miss Collins has placed on my desk. I'll just have to do the best I can – Miss Collins knows I wasn't in the last lesson.

She starts writing the instructions on the board:
You are writing a letter to your French pen-pal called Claudette. Tell her about your holiday by the sea with your family. Mention three things you did whilst on holiday. Also include a description of how you got there and what the weather was like. Don't forget to ask how Claudette's holiday is going.

Oh God. They must have done letter-writing revision last lesson while I was off with my cold. We haven't covered this topic for months. I hope I can remember enough. I start to write, but my hand feels funny, like it's forgotten how to hold a pen properly. *Ma chère Claudette*, I begin clumsily.

What comes next? How do I say, 'I have just come back from holiday'? I write *J'ai juste retourner* . . . what's 'from'? I can only think of *von* in German. Why do they make us take so many languages? And what the hell is 'holiday' in French?

I skip to the next bit. *Ma famille et moi restent prés de la mer.* That doesn't look right either. *Je fais de la natation.* Now I *know* that's not right, I'm using the wrong tense. I squeeze my eyes tight shut, hoping the effort will jog my brain into remembering something useful. When I open my eyes again I see that Marianne has been watching me. She has an expression on her face like she thinks I'm being weird. I glare at her and she turns away.

I look back at my paper but it doesn't make any sense. The writing doesn't look like mine and yet I know I wrote it. What is wrong with me today? Panic rises – a fluttery feeling in my stomach – and I reach under the desk and pinch myself hard on the thigh. I pinch hard enough that I can't think about anything else, and it helps. I feel a bit calmer.

I look down at the paper again. 'Five minutes,' says Miss Collins. Where has the time gone? I scribble as much as I can, not caring about tenses, spelling or punctuation, just wanting to fill the page, fill it up with writing: the writing that doesn't even look like mine.

'How did you do?' mouths Lizzie to me as the papers are collected. I shrug and roll my eyes. She grins sympathetically. 'Sorry. Should have told you.'

'It's OK.' How could I have thought she did it on purpose? She's my friend; she'd never do that to me. I must be paranoid.

'How do you fancy a holiday?' says Mum when she comes back that day. 'Over half-term?'

Anthony's face lights up. 'Yeah! Where?'

'Not sure yet,' says Mum. 'We were thinking about Wales.' She turns to me. 'What do you think?'

What do I think? I think it's a terrible idea. I will miss out on yet more evenings with my friends and will have

64

to spend the whole week with *her*. 'Er . . .' I say, wondering how I can be tactful. Her face falls again and my heart sinks. She thinks this is a great idea. She's really looking forward to it, I can tell. I force my face into a smile. 'It sounds lovely,' I say.

Her face brightens so much that I feel even worse about my non-enthusiasm. 'I'm so pleased you agree, Emily. It might be one of the last family holidays we have, now that you're so much older. And you and Anthony have both been working so hard this term, Dad and I think you need a treat.'

I am the worm on the hook

'*Wales?*' says Lizzie disbelievingly. Marianne gives a snort. 'Why do they want to go to *Wales?*'

I shrug, trying to ignore Marianne's sniggers. 'Dunno. Think they want to do the whole happy-family thing.'

Marianne laughs out loud at this, and I feel myself getting cross. 'What's wrong with that?' I accuse her.

'Nothing,' she says, raising her eyebrows. 'Except that aren't you a bit old for family holidays? Hélène and I are going on holiday by ourselves this year, after the exams. I haven't been on holiday with my parents for *years.*'

'You went to Corfu in the summer,' I say, looking her in the eye.

She flounders for a moment. 'Yeah, but I didn't spend any *time* with them. They just paid for the flights and the hotel and stuff. Anyway, my mum just wanted to snog the face off my stepdad. Yeuch.'

Everyone laughs, and yet again the conversation has turned away from me. Now the focus is back on Marianne. How does she *do* that? What's even cleverer is that she's now got me *defending* my family holiday, when I don't even want to go in the first place!

This puts me in a bad mood for the rest of the day, especially when Lizzie says, 'It's a shame you won't be around for half-term. Marianne and I thought we'd have a sleepover.'

Great. Perfect.

After school we see Hélène waiting at the gates. 'Did you have a good time at the Tavern the other week?' she asks, inhaling the smoke from her cigarette. I don't really know why she's asking: it was ages ago now, and Marianne must have told her we'd had a good night. But she's standing there, one hand resting on her hip, looking the essence of cool.

'Yeah,' says Yasmine appreciatively. 'Thanks so much for getting us in.'

'No problem.' Hélène blows the smoke away. 'I thought you might be interested in the next one.'

'Next one?'

'There's another gig planned. Not for charity or any-thing this time. Some of the boys have formed a rock band. It might be crap but I thought you'd want to come. It'll be harder to sneak you in this time but I've got a mate on the door.'

I wonder briefly how the management at the Tavern is getting away with letting in all these under-age kids, but I guess they don't care as long as they get the money.

'When?' Yasmine is practically drooling.

'First Saturday of half-term. Nine o'clock.'

Lizzie turns to me, concern in her voice. 'Oh, that's a shame, Em. You'll be in Wales.'

Marianne snorts, but when I turn to glare at her she pretends it was a cough and reaches out to take her sister's cigarette. I watch in amazement as she takes a drag. Right outside the school gates. Is she incredibly brave or just incredibly stupid?

'Do you want some?' she asks, holding it out to me.

'What, here?' I ask incredulously.

'Oh, who cares, Emily? Don't be such a square.'

'Go on, Em,' urges Lizzie. 'We all tried it the other night when you weren't there.'

I look around. They are all expectant, eyebrows raised. Marianne is challenging me. I can't possibly back down. This is a test. If I refuse, it'll be another reason for them to leave me out of stuff. Even Hélène is watching me. What has Marianne told her about me? Did they plan this from the beginning? Marianne could have told us about the half-term gig at school. Hélène didn't need to wait for us in person.

My mouth is dry. Quite apart from the fact that I've never smoked, I would never be stupid enough to do it right outside the gates where all the teachers can see.

But I don't have a choice.

I take the cigarette. Marianne sees my hand trembling and smirks. She is the fisherman and I am the worm on the hook, squirming.

I put the cigarette to my lips. It is warm and dry. I take a quick breath in and feel the smoke go down into my lungs. That's fine. The problem comes when I try to breathe out. The back of my throat stings, and my reflex cough sends the smoke up into my nose, making my eyes stream.

'Thanks,' I say in a strangled voice, wiping my eyes as I hand the cigarette back. Marianne and Hélène are sniggering, and the others are unable to keep their faces straight either.

'Your face!' giggles Lizzie.

'Emily Bowyer!'

Instantly my stomach drops through the tarmac. I stand, petrified. Miss Jarrow, the deputy head, stalks up to me. 'I would like a word.' She turns and sweeps back through the car park.

'Oh God,' says Lizzie. 'You're for it now.' She sounds thrilled. 'She's gonna kill you.'

'You'd better go, Emily,' says Marianne. 'Maybe she'll understand it was your first offence. After all, it's obvious that was your first drag.'

As I turn to follow Miss Jarrow, I hear laughter break out behind me.

At that moment, I hate them all enough to stick knives in them. Two in Marianne.

'I am *appalled*,' says Miss Jarrow the minute I step into her office. 'Appalled and disappointed in you, Emily.'

I hang my head in shame. It is the easiest way.

'What did you think you were doing?'

I am not sure whether this is a rhetorical question so I keep quiet.

'Emily! I asked you a question.'

It wasn't rhetorical, then. 'I – er –'

69

'Right outside the school gates too!'

She has carried on. It *was* rhetorical, then. My head is spinning from trying to work out the rules of this conversation.

'I know you girls think you're all grown up now, but the law dictates that you cannot smoke until you are sixteen. Besides that, it is against school rules.'

'I was outside the gates,' I mutter.

'And that makes it all right, does it?' she fumes.

This is another rhetorical question, I am sure.

'Smoking in full view of everyone. In school uniform. Not exactly promoting a good image for the school, is it?'

I stare at the floor. The carpet is the browny-beige colour that so many schools have on their floors. It has age-old stains on it, maybe from spilled cups of coffee from years gone by. Or maybe from children's blood, spilled in years gone by too.

'*Is it?*'

Is what? I have forgotten the question, but from the tone in her voice I guess my reply should be in the negative. 'No, Miss Jarrow.'

She sits back and sighs. 'You're one of our best students, Emily. You're rarely in trouble. Your grades are good. Your GCSE results are expected to be excellent. Don't throw it all away.'

'No, Miss Jarrow.'

Her voice softens a bit. 'I know there can be a lot of work to get through this year. But you just have to keep your head down and get on with it. There's time afterwards for the parties and the experimentation.'

Ridiculously, tears are pricking at the back of my eyes. It must be the cigarette smoke I inhaled. I blink them back crossly.

'Do I make myself clear, Emily?'

'Yes, Miss Jarrow.'

'Right.' She nods, and I am dismissed.

They have all gone by the time I get back to the school gates. It seems none of them cared enough to see if I was OK.

The new girl is at the bus stop again. I've seen her once or twice around school but she's not in any of my classes. She smiles at me, and I feel my face respond automatically.

'I saw what happened. Did you get in trouble?' she asks sympathetically.

I shrug. 'Sort of. Not really.'

'That was mean of them to do that to you,' she says. 'They knew you'd get caught.'

'They didn't do it on purpose,' I say in irritation.

She pulls a face at my sharp tone and sits back, staring at the ground.

I instantly feel guilty for snapping at her. I don't know why I did. She was only voicing exactly what I'd thought myself. So why did I jump down her throat about it?

But she can't criticise my friends like that. She doesn't even *know* us. My friends are – well, they're my *friends*. You don't bitch about your friends behind their backs. Besides, we've had so many good times together, you don't just throw it all away like that.

On the bus on the way home, I feel so many different things. I feel angry with the new girl for making assumptions about the people I care about. I am furious with Marianne and Hélène for setting me up like that. I am cross with Lizzie, Maia and Yasmine, who egged me on even though they knew I would probably get caught. I am angry with Miss Jarrow for going on at me again about the bloody GCSEs and not messing up the most important year of my life.

But most of all I am angry with myself for minding so much about it all. It doesn't matter, I tell myself, but no matter how many times I say it inside my head, it doesn't make any difference. It *does* matter.

It matters because my friends shouldn't be able to push me around like that, but then it's my fault for letting them do it to me in the first place.

It matters because if Miss Jarrow feels like it she could easily ring my parents and tell them she caught me smoking. And then all hell will break loose and my life will not be worth living.

And it matters because the girl at the bus stop was only trying to be nice, and I was rude to her and that's unforgivable.

By the time I get home I am so annoyed with myself that I'm slow to notice something's different.

Mum's home. And so's Anthony. They are sitting at the kitchen table and Anthony's eyes are red. Mum looks annoyed.

'What's going on?' I ask.

'Anthony's been sent home from school,' Mum says sharply.

'Sent home? What for?'

'Swearing at a teacher.'

I blink in astonishment. It sounds impossible. Anthony doesn't swear at anyone, let alone someone in authority. I glance at him but he won't meet my eye. 'Who says?'

'The teacher. And four of his classmates.'

'God.' I put my bag down. 'Has he been suspended?'

'I am here, you know,' Anthony suddenly says. 'I am in the room.'

'OK,' I say. 'Have you been suspended?'

'No.' He looks back down at the table.

There is an awkward pause. 'Why did you swear at your teacher?' I ask finally.

'Because she was yelling at me.'

'Why was she yelling at you?'

'Because I didn't do my homework.'

'Why didn't you do your homework?' I feel like an interviewer.

'Because I couldn't, OK?' Anthony suddenly snaps. 'I tried and I couldn't do it. It was too hard.'

I exchange glances with Mum. She shakes her head. 'The teacher says it was something they did in class. It was all explained. Everyone else knew what to do.'

'Well, everyone else isn't stupid, are they?' muttered Anthony.

'Stupid? What are you talking about?' Mum is genuinely shocked. 'You're not stupid.'

'Yes, I am. I can't do any of it. Even when it's explained like six billion times, I still don't get it. The numbers and the letters all jump around on the page.'

'Jump around? What do you mean?'

Anthony makes a sound of frustration. 'Just that – they jump around. I can't explain it. But they don't make any sense.'

Mum takes a breath and tries to sound reasonable. 'But they didn't used to jump around, did they? You didn't have this problem last year.'

'Yes, I did. I just had longer to do things. And people explained them better. But now people don't explain them at all – or only once. I don't always get it first time round.' Tears are welling up in his eyes. 'Then they shout at me. How come they're allowed to shout at me and I'm not allowed to shout at them? It's not fair.' Letting out a sudden sob, he pushes back his chair and runs out of the kitchen. We hear his footsteps on the stairs and then the slam of his bedroom door.

'What's all that about?' I ask.

Mum puts her head in her hands. 'I don't know what to do. What's wrong with him?'

'Nothing's wrong with him.'

'I don't mean it like that. I mean, how come everyone else can do it and he can't? Do you think he's making it up?'

'No, I don't.' I sit down in Anthony's chair. 'I think he needs extra help. Like before.'

'But you only get extra help if you have learning difficulties.'

'Uh, hello? He's having difficulties learning.'

'But he's not – he doesn't have – *problems*. Not like that.'

'How do you know? Maybe he does and nobody noticed.'

'How could they not notice? At primary school, kids were always getting assessed. Nobody ever suggested Anthony had difficulties. Not real difficulties.'

'Probably because there were so many other kids with worse problems.'

Mum looks at me and I am taken aback by her expression. Her forehead is creased and her eyes are anxious. 'Did I miss something really obvious?' she says quietly. 'Has he got dyslexia or something?'

'I don't know. Doesn't that mean you can't spell?'

She doesn't answer.

I don't sleep at all well that night. I lie awake and stare at the ceiling. Anthony's face, pale and miserable, swims before me. He hardly ate anything for dinner, despite Mum's best efforts. As soon as he was allowed, he went straight back to his room. I peeked round the door later but he was hiding under the duvet and wouldn't come out.

These thoughts bring me back to the scene by the gates today. I have nothing to moan about, *nothing*. So what if some of my friends like to have a laugh at my expense? Does it really matter? Anthony can't even get through the day without feeling like a failure.

I get good grades, I have friends and family. How dare I think I have problems when my little brother spends six hours a day feeling stupid?

it's a shame you won't
be there

The work continues to pile up and I start to get a bit sloppy. A few marks dropped here, an unfinished homework there. I don't tell my parents. They have enough to worry about. By the time we reach half-term, Anthony's school has agreed to have him tested by an educational psychologist. Of course, it'll take weeks – and what's he supposed to do in the meantime?

I start to bite my nails, and the bruises on my thighs from pinching myself increase in number. It's a good thing our PE shorts come down to just above our knees. I change facing the wall, so that no one can see the black, purple and yellow marks on my legs.

In the last week the others start to talk about the gig on the Saturday night at the Tavern. They are all giggly and girly, talking about what to wear and who to flirt with. I am excluded from these conversations. Although I am there, I might as well not be, because nobody asks my opinion. And then Lizzie brings up the subject of the sleepover, which is scheduled for the Wednesday of half-term.

'It's a shame you won't be there,' says Maia to me.

Lizzie turns with a startled look. It's almost as though she's forgotten I exist. 'Oh – yeah. Shame, that.'

I make a face. 'Oh well.'

Lizzie starts talking to Marianne again.

'Maybe you can come to the next one,' says Maia, before turning back to the discussion about whether to have popcorn or marshmallows at the party.

I swallow my disappointment. They don't want me there, it's obvious.

I try, desperately, to persuade my parents to go on holiday without me. This is met with disbelief. 'Leave you behind?' Dad stares. 'We can't do that, you're only fifteen.'

'I'm old enough to look after myself,' I say.

'No, you're not,' says Mum. 'Don't be silly, Emily, of course we're not going without you. Besides, it's all booked now.'

'But –'

'I thought you wanted to come with us?' She's wearing her hurt expression and I know I have lost. I can't bear it when she looks like that.

I press down the part of me that wants to shout *no, I don't want to come with you, I want to spend time with my friends like any normal teenager before I am engulfed in the darkness that is my GCSEs*, and I say, 'Of course I want to come. Forget I said anything.'

Mum smiles and gives me a hug. 'You're going to have a great time, I promise.'

And to start with, it is quite good. They have booked

a little holiday chalet in some woods somewhere, and it's kind of sweet, with wood-panelled walls and a jacuzzi option for the bath. There is lots of fresh air and when the clouds part (not very often) there is a great view across valleys and mountains.

But after three days I have read all the books I have brought. I have not yet done any schoolwork, but I tell myself there is lots of time still. Besides, I need some time off, to relax.

But relax is one thing I can't do. For one, sharing a small space with Mum, Dad and Anthony is starting to get on my nerves. Mum and Dad are behaving like teenagers themselves, kissing and cuddling all over the place. It makes me feel nauseous. For another, there is nothing to *do* here. We go on walks. We visit the local town. That's *it*. There aren't any theme parks or cinemas within reach. It's a twenty-minute drive to get to the nearest supermarket, and the reception on the TV is so bad we can't even get Channel Five, let alone digital.

'What is the matter with you?' Mum asks that night at dinner. 'You've been sulky all day.'

'I have not,' I say, poking at my curry.

'You have. You moaned when I suggested going out this morning, you've done nothing but tut and sigh all day, and you've got a face like a wet Wednesday.'

'It *is* a wet Wednesday,' I point out. 'It's been raining all day.'

'But that's no reason for you to sulk. There's lots we can do even if it's raining.'

'Like what?' I mutter.

'I beg your pardon?'

'Nothing.'

'Honestly, Emily, I can't think what's got into you these past few weeks. You've been sulky and moody and you snap at the least little thing. You should be grateful that we've brought you on a holiday in the middle of the term. Most girls your age are having to stay home and study' – here it comes – 'for their GCSEs.'

I grit my teeth. I will not speak. I will not rise to it.

'As it is, I hope you've been getting down to the work they've set you over the half-term. Just because you're on holiday doesn't mean –'

I push my plate away, slightly harder than I mean to. 'I'm going to bed,' I say. My voice is quiet but inside I am shaking. They are taken aback.

'It's not even eight o'clock,' Dad points out. 'Aren't you going to play Monopoly with us?'

'No thanks,' I say, trying to be polite. 'I'm kind of tired.'

As I put my pyjamas on in the next room, I hear Dad say to Mum, 'Don't go on at her about the schoolwork. I thought we came here to get away from it all.'

Mum's voice is tetchy because she thinks Dad is criticising her. 'I'm not going on at her. She has to appreciate the amount of effort she's got to put into these exams. They're not that far away, you know. And I'm not having her ruin our holiday by being Miss Moody. She's got to learn to grow up a bit and accept her responsibilities.'

I sit on the bed, my eyes burning. I can't do anything right, can I? If I get out and about and enjoy myself, she says I'm not doing enough work. If I chain myself to my desk and work through the night, she says it's not healthy, that I need to take a break.

What the hell am I supposed to do?

I look down and realise I'm pinching myself again. The pain is good; it helps me focus. It makes the hurtful and confusing feelings go away for a bit. I wish they would go away for longer. But I can't pinch any harder.

They knew I didn't want to come. I shouldn't have to keep my feelings inside, should I? I'm just letting them know they have ruined my life, that's all. I sit in the bedroom I share with Anthony and stare out at the view. It is beautiful, but although I have brought my sketchbook with me, I can't even raise the enthusiasm to draw.

Every now and then, Mum or Dad tries to persuade me to go out and do stuff with them. I resist for as long as I can, but it is always Mum's hurt expression that twists my stomach into knots and forces me to go. I wish she wouldn't look like that, it tears me up inside. Can't she understand I just want some time on my own?

As the end of the week draws nearer, Anthony also becomes more withdrawn. It is obvious he is dreading going back to school. He doesn't talk much about it, even to me, but whenever school is mentioned he goes all quiet and this blank expression comes over his face.

We come home the Saturday before school starts again on the Monday. I have not done my half-term homework and I have two feelings about this:

The first feeling is one of not caring. Why should I spend so much time learning all this stuff? Am I really going to need to know Pythagoras' Theorem after this? Does it matter whether I can ask a German person what time the train leaves? And it doesn't make any difference how much work I do because nobody knows what will be on the exam papers. Half of what I learn will be wasted anyway.

The other feeling sneaks around and trips me up whenever I tell myself I don't care. It lurks in my stomach and in my mind. It says to me, 'What's happened to you? You were a model student! You have brains: you are throwing your education away. Don't you know that without GCSEs you will never get a job? You can get As if you try. A B grade is *not good enough*. You are not trying your hardest, you must try harder. *You must do your best.*'

On the Sunday before we go back, the insistent voice wins. I stare at the pile of work in horror. How have I managed not to do any of it? What did I think I was going to do? I can't just go back without the work. I have let myself down. I have not been disciplined enough.

I start to work, feverishly. I must complete everything. I cannot go back tomorrow without the work. I must try my best. I can get the top marks in the class: that's where I should be, the top of the class. I have been there before; I can be there again. But I will not get there without putting in the effort.

Every now and then I have to stop to pinch myself.

The pain makes the frantic 'you're not working fast enough!' voice recede a little and it enables me to focus. If I don't pinch myself, the voice gets louder and louder until it fills my head and I want to curl up into a ball and implode.

'I'm glad to see you working, Emily,' says Mum, bringing me a cup of tea. 'But you should stop for little breaks every now and then, you know. To recharge your brain. It's not good to work for hours straight through.'

'Too bad,' I say. 'I have to get this done before tomorrow.'

'Why didn't you do it earlier in the week?' she says.

I sigh in annoyance. 'Because I didn't feel like it, OK?'

She leaves. The hurt expression is beginning to take over her face. I have to pinch myself again to make the guilt go away.

Pinching is not working so well any more. It doesn't last long enough. But I can't think of anything else to do, so I try pinching other areas. The skin on the back of my hands really hurts when I pinch it, and it's a sharper, more immediate pain, so I try that for a bit. By the time everyone else goes to bed, my hands are red and sore with little raised bumps on them. But I have finished the work.

I go to bed, but I cannot sleep. I am exhausted, but my mind is still in overdrive. Have I done the work properly? It only took me the inside of a day – maybe I haven't done it to the best of my ability? The Eng Lit essay only took me an hour and a half – should it have taken longer? And there were some bits in the German homework that were really hard. Have I answered the questions well enough?

I wonder if Anthony has done any of his half-term homework. I know he's dreading school far more than I am. If the educational psychologist finds that Anthony has learning difficulties, Mum's going to be devastated. She already feels guilty enough about not realising he didn't understand the work. She thought he was just playing up, like his teachers said. On the other hand, if it is all official, then maybe he'll start getting some help. The teachers will have to make sure he gets easier work. I wish I were at the same school so that I could keep an eye on him.

Mixed in with these racing thoughts are pictures: Mum's hurt face, Anthony's miserable I-don't-want-to-go-to-school face, Dad's bemused why-can't-we-all-get-on? face.

Thoughts, pictures, feelings – they all seem to gallop around in my head. One thought follows another with hysterical speed. And colouring everything with grey is the relentless dread of the GCSE work. Tomorrow it will begin again and I will have another mountain to climb, another test to take.

I'm not sure I can cope.

they have changed the rules

I look dreadful when I get ready for school the next day. My eyes are puffy and ringed with purplish shadows. My skin is so pale I look like a ghost.

'You're looking a bit peaky today,' says Mum at breakfast.

I glare. 'I'm fine. Just a bit tired, that's all.'

'You must try not to stress about your exams so much,' she says. 'Stress prevents our brains from functioning properly. You have to stay focused and not let yourself get stressed.'

I do not bother to reply to this. I am in a mood because I have just realised that Lizzie never rang me yesterday. She knew what day I was getting back from Wales. Why didn't she call?

Anthony says he has a stomach ache and can't go to school. Mum is sympathetic but she won't let him stay home. He sulks all through breakfast.

I see the new girl on the bus on the way into school. I still feel bad about snapping at her the week before half-term, so I go to sit next to her. She looks up, surprised.

'Can I sit here?'

'If you like.'

I cram my bag onto my lap. 'Did you have a good half-term?'

There is a slight pause, and then she says, 'It was all right.'

There's another pause, and I feel it's really time for me to apologise. 'Look, I'm sorry I was rude to you. That day I got caught by Miss Jarrow. I was just annoyed with myself.'

She smiles at me. 'That's OK. I do that sometimes too – get annoyed with myself, I mean.'

I nod. 'Life sucks sometimes.'

'Yeah.'

When we get off the bus at school, I realise I still don't know her name.

I am ridiculously pleased to see Lizzie and the others. I have missed them so much. Perhaps I am a little over-enthusiastic, because Lizzie looks slightly put out by my excitement.

'Oh, hi, Em.'

'Well?' I say. 'How was half-term? How was the gig at the Tavern?'

'The Tavern?' she says slowly, frowning.

Marianne breaks in. 'That was *ages* ago.'

'Only a week last Saturday,' I argue. 'Anyway –' I turn pointedly back to Lizzie. 'What was it like?'

She shrugs. 'It was OK, I guess. Can't remember much. We all got pretty drunk.'

'What about the sleepover, did you manage to have one?'

She gives me a cool look, and I feel a slight chill. Have I asked the wrong question? 'It was really good,' she says finally, as though bored. I wait for her to say 'shame you weren't there', but she doesn't.

I try to ask another question, but Mr Simmons, our form teacher, tells me to be quiet. Marianne smirks. Maia winks at me, and I feel such a rush of warmth towards her it's embarrassing.

At break, Maia tells me a bit about the sleepover. 'It was OK,' she says, 'but Lizzie's parents kept arguing. I felt kind of weird.'

'I feel like that around them,' I agree. 'My parents don't argue much.'

'Mine neither. But at least Lizzie's parents don't seem to be on at her all the time. About work, I mean.'

'Do your parents do that too?' I say eagerly. 'I mean, mine are always asking, over and over again – How was school? How are your grades? Are you doing enough work? Why are you having a five-minute break? And then, just when I think I have it figured, they want to know why I'm looking so tired all the time, and am I getting enough sleep? I mean, you just can't win, can you?'

Maia is looking at me in some alarm. 'Er – no, I guess.'

My stomach jolts. 'Don't yours do that to you?'

'Well, yeah.' She shrugs. 'I think it's kind of normal for parents. I just tell them it's none of their business.'

'Maia!' Yasmine calls over. 'I'm going to the tuck shop, do you want anything?'

'Oh yeah!' calls back Maia. Is she looking relieved? 'I'll come with you!' She hastily leaves.

I have the feeling I did something wrong again. I shouldn't have shouted my mouth off about my parents. She thinks I'm moaning. I should have just been sympathetic and kept my mouth shut. That's what makes a good friend, right? Someone who listens?

But her reply bothers me. 'I just tell them it's none of their business.' I can't imagine ever saying that to my mum. She'd have a fit. I can just hear her response. 'What do you mean, it's none of my business? Of course it's my business; everything you do while you're under my roof is my business. How dare you talk to me like that?' And then her face would drop. 'I'm sorry, Emily,' she'd say. 'I don't seem to be able to do anything right any more. Why can't you just talk to me? I might be able to make it better, whatever it is.'

No, I could never say something like that to her. I envy Maia for her cool demeanour. And the way she can handle everything. She always seems so calm. I wish I could be like that.

'I know it's still the end of October, but we only have five weeks before your mocks begin,' says Mrs Begum by way of a preamble. 'You may have forgotten how to work over the half-term holiday. I'm here to remind you.'

And remind us she does. Reminds me just how little I know about Pythagoras' Theorem and how to calculate the area of a circle. Of course, it all comes back, but only after several examples. And I get this horrible feeling – what if there's a question on the mock paper that

I haven't revised? I don't have time to practise a bit before answering the question. I am going to have to revise everything I have learned over the past year and a half in order to be able to answer a handful of questions.

And so the day goes on. And each subject teacher reminds us of just how little time we have left – how they can't be expected to hold our hands through the revision period, how it's time to take responsibility for our own learning. And each time someone mentions 'mocks' the tight knot of worry in my stomach gets a little bigger.

Lizzie is speaking to me at lunchtime, but I am so wrapped up in my worry I don't hear her the first time. 'I'm sorry, what did you say?'

She rolls her eyes. 'For God's sake, Em, what's the matter with you at the moment? Did you leave your brain behind in Wales?'

Marianne, ever-present, snorts with laughter. I don't have a reply. My mouth opens as if to speak, but closes again, foolishly.

Lizzie shakes her head. 'Oh, forget it.' She walks away.

I want to call after her, to replay the conversation, to have a second chance. But I cannot move. What is going on? Have I changed or have they? Something is different. It is as though suddenly the rules are no longer the same. While I was away they have changed the rules and I don't know what the new ones are and they won't tell me.

I get my head down for the rest of the day and barely speak to anyone. There is no point. I will get it wrong again and they will laugh at me. Better to say nothing.

The girl is there at the bus stop and I automatically

move towards her.

'How was yours?'

She wrinkles her nose.

'Mine too.'

She has a bandage on her wrist, I notice, but I don't ask why. Instead, I tell her about the non-conversation at lunchtime. She listens and nods.

'That happened to me at my old school. That's why I left. It always starts the same way. You be careful. That's why I don't make friends any more. Too much hassle.'

I'm a bit offended that she doesn't think I'm a friend, but then I realise I don't think of her as a friend either. Not yet anyway. You can't be friends with someone just like that.

'Where was your old school?'

She wrinkles her nose. 'Not round here. In a different county.'

'Oh.'

There is a pause. 'What's your name?' I remember to ask.

She looks surprised. 'I thought you knew it. It's Patrice. You're Emily, aren't you?'

'Yes.'

We sit in silence for the rest of the journey.

Anthony says his day was OK, but this mostly seems to be because he had PE and Music – two subjects which don't require much reading or writing. I'm beginning to spot a pattern.

'How was school?' Mum asks me.

I shrug. 'All right. Got to go and do my homework, though.'

'How long is it till mocks?'

I freeze on the stairs. 'Five weeks.'

She breathes out. 'Whew. Not long, is it? Amazing how it can just creep up on you.'

Amazing.

I start to move again, but she hasn't finished.

'Well, if there's anything you need, don't be afraid to ask. I was quite good at French in my day,' she winks.

I force a smile. 'Thanks. I think I can manage.'

'I'll bring you up a cup of tea.'

'OK.'

Back in my room, the paperwork looms like a white fog covering my desk. I sit and stare at it. I don't know where to start. The week off has vanished into a puff of smoke – it is as though the holiday never existed. Just the endless, mindless road of textbooks and worksheets. Leading to the dark, grey and choking smog of exams. And then more exams. As if GCSEs weren't bad enough, they make you do them twice. And instead of saying, 'The mocks are just practice, try not to worry about them,' the teachers pile so much pressure on you the mocks might as well be the real thing. 'If you revise hard for the mocks, then you only have half the work to do for the real thing,' they say encouragingly. 'But you must work as hard as possible, because if you do badly in the mocks, it's nearly impossible to pull yourself back up.'

Thanks. I feel so much better.

new strategy

Before I know it, it's November. I have been working hard, keeping my head down, just trying to get through each day. I have given up initiating conversations with Lizzie and the others. Instead I have worked out a new strategy. It goes like this:

1. Look friendly but not over-happy.
2. On no account look sad or depressed.
3. Sympathise with every sob story.
4. Agree with every opinion expressed by Lizzie and Marianne.
5. Never express my own opinion, unless in private to Patrice.
6. Give the impression that I am working hard and that my parents won't let me go out in the evenings. This makes it easier to cope when they don't invite me.

It is working but I am exhausted. The effort of having to look cheerful all the time is wearing me down on the inside. My cheek and forehead muscles have started to ache from all the sympathetic listening and agreeing I'm doing. I am not sure I can keep it up for much longer.

Things come to a head on the fifth. It is nearly Lizzie's birthday and I haven't heard anything more since she suggested the Alton Towers trip. I suppose in a small way I have actually forgotten about it. But when I go up to the group at lunchtime I overhear them discussing it.

'My dad said he'll borrow the minibus from work,' Marianne is saying. Everyone else is looking excited.

'That's brilliant!' Lizzie says. 'Then we can easily fit everyone in. We could even invite a couple more people. What about Hélène, Marianne? She did us a favour with the Tavern gigs.'

Marianne grins. 'I'll ask her, but she's got a new boyfriend at the moment and they're practically joined at the groin.'

I quietly join the group, my 'friendly and interested' expression fixed on my face. Lizzie immediately starts giving the others signals with her eyes. Marianne shuts her mouth with an audible snap. Yasmine nods and looks at the ground.

Maia misses the visual instruction. She turns to me and smiles. 'Hi, Em. We were just talking about Lizzie's birthday. Will your parents let you come?'

An icy tingle begins at my scalp and spreads down my neck and arms. For a moment I feel dizzy. There is a silence. Maia's expression changes to puzzlement. I turn to gaze at Lizzie and stare coolly into her eyes. To my secret pleasure, she looks very uncomfortable.

'Er . . . Emily . . .' She stops to clear her throat and starts again. 'I – er – I didn't ask you because . . .'

I fix my 'friendly and interested' expression even more firmly onto my face. I must not crack. I am terribly afraid I might cry. I want to say something sardonic, but there is too much of a danger that opening my mouth will break my concentration.

Lizzie looks helplessly at Marianne, but she is on her own this time. No one else will meet her eye.

'I didn't think your parents would let you come,' she says finally. Even to me it sounds lame.

'Oh really?' I say. 'And how would I know what their answer is if I never ask them the question?'

Lizzie rolls her eyes (she's getting good at that) and says impatiently, 'I didn't really think you'd be interested, Emily. You always have your head stuck in your books these days. I thought you'd be revising.'

'Oh,' I say, and the anger that is growing inside me gives me courage to speak. 'So which is it, Lizzie? You didn't think my parents would let me come, or you didn't think I'd be interested, or I'd be too busy revising? That seems like an awful lot of reasons not to ask me. Are you sure you didn't miss out the most important one?'

She turns to Marianne, and an expression passes between them. I know what it means: it means 'Oh, here we go. Emily's going to make a scene. Let's watch her make a fool of herself.'

I know this is what they are thinking, but it just makes me even angrier. 'Are you sure those are the reasons, Lizzie? Because it sounds to me like you just didn't want me there. At all.' Now that I have opened my mouth I can't close it again. 'I mean, you've invited lots of other people by the sounds of it – hell, you've even invited Marianne's *sister*. There would have been room in the van. But no, you just don't want me around any more, do you? Because now you've found yourself a *new* friend. And *isn't she pleased*?' I snarl at Marianne. She is trying not to smile. I want to smack her in the face. 'Well, fine, Lizzie, if you want to throw away five years of friendship, then it's your loss. I used to think you were a good friend, but I guess I was wrong.' I shake my head.

But Lizzie has heard enough.

'How *dare* you?' she suddenly explodes. Marianne's smirk is wiped off in an instant. 'How dare you lecture *me* on being a good friend? You never call me, you don't even look as though you're interested in talking to me any more. You used to be a laugh – now you're just a drag. All you ever do is *moan*. You want to know why I didn't invite you, Emily? You really want to know?' She's right in my face now, and it's all I can do not to grip her round the neck or punch her lights out. 'I didn't invite you, Emily, because I wanted my birthday to be *fun*. You always ruin things – "I have to go home early, you shouldn't be smoking that" – I don't want to hear it! You're so perfect, so clever, so I-am-always-right with that smug expression on your face. You think you're so much better than everyone else. Well, let me tell you something, Emily Bowyer. You are *nothing*. You are *nobody*. You are dull and boring and you have no life!'

'I do have a life!' I scream back. My brain has no control over my mouth now. I am screaming and she is screaming, and Marianne is smiling again because Lizzie is winning. And then I look round and see everyone's shocked faces and Miss Jarrow storming through the door with a thunderous look on her face, and I turn and run.

I run and run without any thought as to where I'm going. I end up outside by the bike shed.

I feel very sick. The back of my throat is burning and it's not from the shouting. My body is starting to shake and I hold out my hand in front of me to see it tremble. There is a sort of white swirling mist in my head, full of accusations and noise and blame. There are so many feelings, I can't deal with them. They are overwhelming me.

I cannot cry. I want to but I don't want to. If I cry they will have won. And it will also mean that I am admitting that I am all those things: I am dull; I am boring; I have no life. But I thought that's what everyone *wanted* me to be. Isn't it?

I do not look at anyone for the rest of the afternoon. Miss Jarrow calls me into her office again and gives me a short, sharp lecture on decorum. I nod, staring at the floor. I am too tired to argue. There is no point anyway. Eventually she gives up, disgusted.

Patrice is not at the bus stop. I sit next to a fat Year Eight, who eats a doughnut and drops jam on my skirt.

When I get to my room, I realise I have no recollection of opening the front door or walking up the stairs. But I must have done so, otherwise I wouldn't be here.

Now I am losing my mind as well as my friends.

There is a feeling inside me like an ache. It swirls from my stomach to my arms, to my neck, right down to my feet and back again. It is as though I am made of fog. It is a fog of feelings – feelings that are so numerous and painful that I cannot tell which is which. They are taking me over. I am no longer a person. I am a vessel for emotions. They hurt me from the inside – not the pain that you get from an injury or a bruise – a formless, nameless pain that permeates every cell.

My body is screaming.

I reach to pinch my hand, but the slight pain on the outside is a drop in the ocean. It cannot possibly drive back the tide. It is like rowing a boat in a storm. The storm is so huge, it will engulf my little dinghy.

I look down at my desk. There are pens, pencils, a ruler. And a pencil sharpener.

There is a blade in my pencil sharpener. It cuts pencils.

Methodically I unscrew the blade using the tip of my ruler. It pops out with a 'ping', and I pick it up, wonderingly. I wipe it carefully on a tissue. I don't want to get lead poisoning, although I know really that pencils aren't made with lead any more.

I take the blade in my right hand and I spread my left hand out on the desk. The swirling fog is hesitating, as if in anticipation. For this moment in time, I am calm. I know what I am about to do.

I draw the blade across the back of my left hand.

96

It leaves a sharp red line, like a cat scratch.

It also hurts.

And, miraculously, the fog of emotion starts to recede. It is as though the sun has come out and is burning the mist away. My body stops screaming. I stare at the mark on my hand.

My pain is real now.

I can see it.

Others can see it.

Therefore, I am not mad.

I take a deep shuddering breath. I can feel the air rushing into my lungs, seeping into my bloodstream. The sharpness of the pain in my hand ebbs and leaves a slight sting. Tiny beads of blood form, but they quickly clot.

My mouth curves in a smile. On the inside I feel euphoric, like I have just sniffed cocaine. I mean, I've never sniffed cocaine, but I imagine this is what it's like. My body is still exhausted, but now it is calm. My hand stings a bit but my mind can work again. It is no longer being controlled by those horrible feelings. It can sort, categorise and prioritise.

And now my priority is my homework. I take out my books and start, glancing at my hand every now and then for reassurance. It must have been bad, that I could do that to myself, mustn't it?

When Mum comes in with Anthony, I greet her with a smile. She looks surprised but pleased. 'Did you have a good day?' she asks.

'Yes,' I reply.

idiot

In the morning, I wake with a dull pain in my left hand.
It is a moment before I remember why. I lie in bed and
gaze at the long red scratch. But instead of feeling
euphoric, I feel stupid. What on earth was I thinking? I
deliberately hurt myself with a blade from a pencil
sharpener, for God's sake. What kind of idiot would do
that?

I shake my head. I must have been crazy last night.
But I did my homework, so that's the most important
thing.

I pull the sleeves of my jumper down over my hands.
Mum doesn't notice.

Patrice notices, though, on the bus. 'Ouch, how did you
do that?' she exclaims.

I blush. 'Oh – the cat did it.'

'Nasty.'

'It'll be all right.'

'We used to have a cat ...' she trails off.

I look at her sympathetically. 'What happened?'

Her mouth tightens oddly. 'It got run over.'

'You poor thing,' I say, feeling terribly sad for her. 'You must have been really upset.'

'Yeah.'

She doesn't say any more.

I smile at Maia in registration, but she looks away quickly. I frown. Lizzie and Marianne walk past with no sign of having noticed me. Yasmine looks at them, and then at me. But when I catch her eye, she too looks quickly away.

On the way to Maths I try to speak to Maia. 'How's it going?' I ask.

She looks slightly flustered, and goes to answer me, but then changes her mind and clamps her mouth shut. She won't meet my gaze.

What is going on?

As the morning wears on, it is not hard to work out. They've all agreed to pretend I'm invisible. I can tell that Lizzie and Marianne are behind it, and that Maia and Yasmine are just doing what they're told, but the chill of their hostility makes me shiver.

I have never had no one to talk to at lunch before. They walk past me, and Lizzie raises her nose and sniffs loudly. 'Is there a funny smell round here?' she asks. Marianne erupts into giggles. I pretend I haven't heard.

I sit alone at a table. Every mouthful seems to take for ever. I wish I had brought a book to read – then I could have looked purposeful. Instead I just look sad – Norma No-Mates. There isn't even another group I can join.

Everyone has been divided into cliques for years. Moving from one to another is unthinkable.

In afternoon lessons, I don't attempt to speak to anyone. There is no point. I would just be frozen out again.

I think I get through the afternoon without uttering a single word. Even the teachers do not notice me.

The week continues like this. I wonder whether Lizzie and the others will become tired of the game, but they show no signs of giving it up. Apart from Patrice, I have no one to talk to.

I become a loner – a nobody. I spend time in the library, flicking through books I have no interest in. I do not volunteer answers in class, and when the teacher asks me a question, I give the shortest, quietest answer possible. I go from one lesson to another looking at the ground; making eye contact with nobody. I do my work diligently and with concentration.

Between eight fifty-five a.m. and three thirty-five p.m. I am completely invisible.

'You should do something,' says Patrice.

'Like what?' I am bored with this conversation. We have had it three times already this week.

'Tell someone. A teacher. Your form tutor.'

'Mr Simmons? Don't make me laugh. He won't care. And what could he do anyway?'

'Miss Jarrow, then.'

I repress a shudder. I can just imagine her summoning us all into her office and ordering us to be friends.

Lizzie shaking my hand with a sneer. All of us filing out, and then . . .

'That would just make things worse,' I say. 'You know there isn't anything they could do. I just have to keep my head down and try not to get in their way.'

Patrice looks at me, troubled. 'You look terrible,' she says.

'Thanks.'

'You've got these dark circles under your eyes and you look really pale.'

I'm not surprised, I'm hardly getting any sleep. I just lie awake at night looking at the ceiling.

'Have you told your mum?'

'No.' Mum has enough to worry about at the moment. The date for Anthony's educational assessment has come through. 'I can't talk to her.'

Patrice shakes her head in despair. 'You have to do something, Emily. You can't go on like this.'

Can't I? I don't know, Patrice, maybe I can.

I am discovering that it is possible to exist without living.

It is strange, but I never imagined my life could be so turned around in the blink of an eye. I suppose this is what homeless people go through: lose job, get thrown out of house, look back and think, 'How did that happen to me?' But at least they would get a bit more warning – a time to become accustomed to the thought that life is changing.

I have had no such warning. Last week, yesterday, an

hour ago – or at least, it feels that recent – my life was like *that*. But that was before.

This is after.

And what I can't work out is – how did I get from then to now?

I suppose it seems as though I am being very philosophical. And on the outside, I am. I am intellectually calm about this. I argued with Lizzie. I am being punished.

That is logical.

Mum and Dad have not noticed. They are worried about Anthony. Well, Mum is worried, and she makes sure Dad worries too. And they assume that I will tell them if I have a problem, or something on my mind. Because I have always done so in the past. And then we have talked it through. Rationally, calmly. Without strong feelings or anxiety.

It is logical that they should assume this.

My teachers are pleased that I am devoting more time to my studies. They don't care particularly that I don't sit with my not-friends any more. They think I am concentrating harder on my work.

It is logical that they wouldn't care.

But inside me, in the part which is not controlled by logic or reason, I am crying. Quietly, silently. No one can see it, but it is there. My insides are being washed with tears.

I am not hysterical.

Hysteria is short-lived.

This crying can last for ever.

Mum says to me after that first dreadful week, 'Are you

all right? You seem very quiet at the moment.'

I give a rueful grin. 'Oh, you know. Just working. Trying to get my head round everything.'

She gives me a hug. 'I know it's hard, darling. Just think – only a few more months to go. Then we'll have a real party, hmm?'

'Yeah.' I hug her back, but my spirit is not lifted. It is so far in darkness that a simple hug will never bring it back. 'Well, better get on with my revision.'

'It's Friday night. Why don't you take the night off? Aren't your friends going out tonight?'

Yes, they are. They are all going to Destiny, and then having a sleepover at Lizzie's before her birthday trip tomorrow. I only know because Chantelle in Art told me. I have not spoken to a single one of them for four days. I shrug. 'Not sure. Think they're revising too.'

She raises her eyebrows. 'Doesn't sound like Lizzie.'

'Um.'

She peers at me, concerned. 'Is everything all right, Emily?'

I shake her hands off me, suddenly irritated. 'I'm *fine*, Mum, just stop asking. I've got work to do.' I turn so that I don't have to see her face.

I go to my room and shut the door. But no sooner have I sat at my desk than there is a faint knocking.

'I said leave me *alone*!' I snap.

'Oh,' says a small voice. 'Sorry.' It's Anthony, and he goes away.

I feel dreadful. I should get up and call after him. He probably wants to talk about his assessment. But I can't lift my arms and legs; it's too much effort. I open my mouth to call, but I can't even speak. Instead I put my head on the desk and close my eyes.

Dad tries to talk to me over dinner. I can tell Mum's asked him to, because she keeps giving him little signals with her eyes.

'Emily, we're worried about you,' he says, as I slice into my jacket potato. I don't know what to say, so I don't say anything. He sighs.

'You seem very withdrawn at the moment. Has something happened? Something at school?'

I shake my head, concentrating on spreading butter on the potato. Dad looks at Mum. Mum looks frustrated. Anthony looks curious.

'What about your friends?' Mum blurts out. 'We haven't seen much of them recently – have you fallen out?'

Fallen out? Fallen out of what? What a ridiculous expression.

I look at her, and then I look at Dad. I can't bear to look at Anthony, I might cry. What can I say? How can I possibly explain this darkness that is taking me over? How can I tell them about the numb pain that engulfs me? About the effort of living minute to minute – second to second? There is nothing they could do anyway, and I can just imagine their expressions. It would make me feel even worse than I already do.

'Oh, it's nothing really. We had a bit of an argument, but things are OK now. I'm just really tired.' I give them a weak smile.

They are starting to look relieved, so I add a bit more.

'The mocks, you know . . .'

They nod understandingly. 'We understand,' says Dad.

'All friendships go through difficult patches,' says Mum.

'And you are working very hard.'

'Just remember we love you.'

Thanks. I'm sure that'll help a lot.

Anthony comes to visit me later in his pyjamas. He doesn't say anything, he just gives me a hug.

When he goes, I cry for half an hour. But it doesn't help.

you're only a victim so long as you choose to be

Over the next week, my 'friends' step up the campaign.

On the way to Maths, Lizzie trips me up.

In French, Marianne 'accidentally' squirts ink from her cartridge all over my hands.

When we are asked to work in groups for English Language, I am the only one not in a group. The teacher asks Yasmine if I can join their group. Yasmine hesitates and looks at Lizzie. Lizzie says no. Very firmly. The teacher is surprised, but puts me in a different group. They are all polite but in a not-very-friendly way, and I don't know the in-jokes. I feel like a spare part. There is lots of giggling and laughing from Lizzie's table.

On Wednesday, I get back after lunch to find my locker has been broken into and filled with grass from the playground. Mr Simmons tells me off for making a mess. When I try to explain, he says to me, 'For goodness' sake, Emily, can't you sort this out yourself? You're only a victim so long as you choose to be.'

Lizzie and Marianne are sniggering from their desks.

I stare at Mr Simmons, hating him with every fibre of my being. If my stare had any power, it would vaporise him on the spot. How can he say that? I'm *choosing* to be a victim? I'm *choosing* to be sniggered at; to be tripped up; to have my equipment destroyed? I feel like screaming at him: *How dare you say this is my fault?*

But of course I don't, and he walks away.

Patrice is away again. I wonder vaguely why – she seems to get ill at the drop of a hat. On the bus, some girls from our year catch sight of me and start whispering behind their hands. I can't hear what they're saying, but it's obvious it's about me because they keep darting looks at me. They get off before me, and as the last one passes me, she says, daringly, 'Swot.'

I sit, my face burning. The Year Seven girl next to me looks at me curiously and then returns to her book.

The word echoes through my head. *Swot, swot, swot, swot . . .*

It takes over my body, fills it with hatred. The disease is spreading. Now not only my friends hate me, but they are infecting everyone else in my year. Soon no one will acknowledge me.

My life is crumbling.

When I get home, I go straight to the kitchen drawer and select a sharp knife. I take it upstairs with me.

I am afraid this time. The knife is larger than the blade from my pencil sharpener, so it's harder to control. I must be very careful.

And I mustn't cut my hand again. It's too obvious a

place. Even Mum noticed in the end, although I said I'd scraped it on my locker.

I look at myself carefully in the mirror. Which place will be easiest to conceal? I take off my shirt and prod my arms experimentally. Lower arms are too risky – we wear T-shirts in PE. Upper arms are probably best.

I take the knife in my hand and carefully draw it across the skin. It stings, and there is a little more blood than last time, but the cut is cleaner. I put the knife down and exhale. Serenity floods through my body.

That's better.

When you have no one to talk to, there is nothing to mark the days. There is nothing to look back on and say, 'Oh, that happened on Tuesday.' My day is marked out by the lessons I go to and nothing else. Patrice is not in any of my classes, so I can't sit with her. I sit on my own wherever possible. Lizzie and Marianne have taken to passing notes around the class about me. I intercept one in French. It has a crudely drawn cartoon of me with enormous spectacles and millions of books. The word SWOT is written on my forehead.

Miss Collins keeps me behind.

'Emily, what's going on? You all used to be such good friends. What happened?'

I shrug. 'Don't know.'

'I don't like seeing you so miserable. Now is not the time to be going through problems with friends. The mocks are next week. Are you managing all right?'

I nod, staring at her desk. There is a shiny new pencil

waiting to be sharpened for the first time.

'Emily?'

She waits, but I can't say anything. There is nothing to say.

'Is everything all right at home?'

I nod.

'Do your parents know about this situation with your friends?'

I shake my head.

'I really think you should tell them, Emily.'

'I can't,' I say. 'They're worried about my brother. He has learning difficulties.'

She sighs. 'Well, you know I'm here if you need anything. I don't like this situation, Emily. I don't like it at all. It's tantamount to bullying.'

It takes a while for this to sink in. I suppose, deep down, I know she's right, but it doesn't feel like it. Bullying? Surely that's when people beat you up, steal your lunch money, pull your hair? My friends have stopped speaking to me – so what? Why am I making this into such a big deal? And even if Miss Collins is right, everyone gets bullied, don't they? It's something you go through; part of childhood. It happened a bit at primary school. Some kids decided to follow me to school for a week, calling me nasty names. Then they got bored and moved on to someone else.

Why should it be any different this time?

And how come everyone else gets through it all right and I have resorted to cutting myself?

There. I said it. I am cutting myself because my friends are not speaking to me. And because I am worried about the exams.

How pathetic am I? I find myself blushing in the lunch hall for no reason at all. I can't meet anyone's eye. What would they say if they knew? I am a pathetic loser who goes home to make scratches in her own skin. I am so weak I can't even cope with a few tests. No wonder no one wants to be my friend. They probably saw through me a long time ago. Who would want to be friends with someone like me? Someone so weak she can't even stand up for herself?

What has happened to me?

The mocks start. I am numb with terror. Every night I sit and stare at my books, but nothing goes into my head. I try everything you're supposed to do: I revise for twenty minutes at a time, then walk around my room or have a glass of water. I divide my time up into revision topics – giving the longest time to the ones I know least well. I go to bed at a reasonable time.

None of this works. When I 'revise' I find that no matter how many times I read a passage, I cannot remember a word of it. More often, I find that twenty minutes have gone by and I have not actually read a word. I have been staring into space.

The exam room makes me feel sick every time I walk into it. The paper lying in front of me, face down, contains humiliation. I know this because when I turn it over, the questions make no sense. I am not used to this:

I have always been good at exams – I am a top student! I try to dredge up my concentration, but even reading the exam paper takes so much effort I have none left to write my answers.

The exams last a week. I know perfectly well that this time I have disgraced myself. I have not read the questions properly, nor answered them correctly. I have left gaps on the paper where my brain would not provide even a glimpse of the information I need.

Mum and Dad have taken to treating me as though I were bone china. I catch them glancing at me when I eat dinner. Mum used to ask how things were going, but I jumped down her throat so many times, she doesn't dare now.

I am driving my family away as well as my friends.

And the excruciating thing is: inside, I am crying out for someone to help me. But I can't tell them. Why can't they see it?

It's probably for the best. If they could see what I am really like inside, they wouldn't want to know me anyway.

don't spoil it

When mocks finally finish, the term ends. In a way, I am relieved not to have to face the wall of silence any more. The rest of the class has become bored with whispering about me, but Lizzie, Marianne, Maia and Yasmine still do not speak to me.

I have cut six times now. I suppose soon I will lose count. It helps, although the effects don't last very long. Still, they last long enough to get me through the darkest times. It is only in the morning I feel incredibly stupid.

Mum is thrilled that the holidays are here. The educational psychologist's report arrives during the last week of term, and it's clear Anthony has moderate learning difficulties. I'm surprised at the way she takes it – she seems relieved. But I guess she's had a long time to come to terms with the idea, and at least it means that he'll get extra help at school. The school has promised that they will appoint a learning support assistant next term. They stopped putting him in detention for not doing his homework after Mum complained.

So all in all, Mum is looking forward to having us both at home all day. To start with, she arranges a trip to the cinema to see the latest animated comedy. It's the first family trip we've had since half-term, and I find it surprisingly nice. It makes a change to spend time with people who actually like me.

The film is hilarious. I haven't laughed like that for – a month? Feels like a year. For two hours I manage to forget all the unpleasant things that have been happening. I forget the nasty comments, the sneaky glances, the sniggers. I am completely absorbed in the film.

We all come out smiling. 'That was great,' says Mum.

Anthony giggles. 'I liked the bit where they were all hanging off the cliff and the monkey farted.'

'I liked the bit where the handsome prince got squashed behind the door,' I say.

'I liked that bit too,' says Mum, smiling at me. She gives me a hug. 'It's good to see you looking happy for a change.'

You know that thing where you make that whistling noise of a bomb falling? That's what my insides start to do when she says that. Suddenly, all the things that have just made me laugh so hard don't seem funny any more. The bit where the prince gets squashed behind the door? Not raising a smile this time.

Mum doesn't notice, and they all carry on happily chatting all the way to the car. I trail behind, trying to work out why all of a sudden I feel fed up. I was so high on the film – how can I suddenly feel so down?

In the car, Dad suddenly says, 'It's really nice to do

something as a family for once. I've really enjoyed this evening.'

'Me too,' says Mum.

'Me too,' squeaks Anthony.

'We should do this again,' says Dad. 'What do you think?'

Anthony says 'yeah!' enthusiastically. Mum twists round to look at me.

'What do you think, Emily?'

I shrug. 'Yeah, whatever.'

Her forehead creases. 'What's the matter?'

I shake my head crossly. 'Nothing.'

'You were really happy a minute ago. You were laughing and smiling and having a good time. Come on. Don't spoil it.'

Don't spoil it? *Don't spoil it?*

'I'm not,' I say irritably.

'Yes, you are. Why can't you just admit you're having a good time for once? You've been such a grump the last few weeks. And we make the effort to take you out and now you're determined to be miserable again. Why can't you just pull yourself together, Emily?'

'Oh, for God's sake!' I explode. Dad swerves in the road. 'Why are you making such a big deal out of it? I didn't *ask* you to take me out, did I?'

Her mouth sets in a thin line. 'Fine. We won't make the effort next time.'

'Fine. I'd rather be left alone anyway.'

She turns round in her seat again and we drive home in stony silence. Anthony is sneaking glances at me, but

I won't look at him.

I am a horrible person.

I am sent to my room in disgrace. Well, that's not quite accurate. I go to my room voluntarily rather than sit with Stone Mum. She is determined not to look at me or communicate in any way. I wonder if there is a conspiracy in the world. That eventually there will be no one left who will acknowledge my existence. If that happened, would I cease to exist too?

I would like to be invisible. If you are invisible you don't have to deal with people. You don't have to pretend to be something you're not. You don't have to fit in with their silly preconceptions of you. I am tired of trying to do and be what everyone else wants. What about what I want?

But it doesn't matter what I want. I know that. I am such a horrible person I don't deserve to get what I want anyway. Look at the way I just behaved. Mum and Dad are good parents. Anthony is a nice brother. Why am I determined to mess things up for us?

I want to cut, but there's nothing in the room to use. I don't want to use the blade from my pencil sharpener again, it's too fiddly. The kitchen knives are all downstairs, of course. I have been cleaning them carefully and putting them back. Scissors? But I don't have any in the room.

It doesn't cross my mind to do anything else. There is nothing else that will work, that will take away this awful feeling. Besides, I deserve to punish myself for the horrible things I said.

I have an idea and go into the bathroom. Mum keeps nail scissors by the basin. But when I get in there, I catch sight of her disposable razor on the side of the bath. She always buys the cheap ones, unlike me. She says they work just as well, but I tried to use hers once and cut my leg by accident. Since then I've used the safety razors. Now I'm glad she uses disposables. I get a new one out of the bathroom cupboard and take it back to my room.

It's tricky to use, and much harder to cut myself on purpose than I thought. I do manage a couple of paper-type cuts, but they don't do the job properly. In the end, I bash it with a folder to break the plastic surround. Then I take the blade out.

I lay out my tissues and roll up my sleeve. There is a neat row of scars on my upper arm. Some are healed over; others are still red and sore. I select an unmarked area.

It takes Mum a long time to forgive me for the cinema trip. She doesn't speak to me unless absolutely necessary, and when she does it's in an icily polite voice, as though I am a stranger and not her own daughter. Dad is perplexed. He tries to make the peace a couple of times, but both Mum and I are so unhelpful that he gives up.

Anthony is bothered to start with, but the fact that school is over for a whole two and a half weeks brings a smile to his face. Plus, of course, there is always Christmas.

Christmas. I've always loved Christmas, ever since I was a small child, but somehow this year I can't summon up any enthusiasm. Maybe I'm getting too old for Christmas – Mum always said it was for children. I suppose I'm not a child any more, although sometimes I wish I were. Things were simpler then.

Three days before Christmas Day, we put up the decorations. I haven't cut since the cinema episode – the intense feelings of hopelessness have subsided for now.

Dad gets excited by decorating. We choose a tree from Sainsbury's, and he carefully wedges it in the red pot we always use. Then he puts on the lights. Then it's our turn, mine and Anthony's, to deck it in tinsel and baubles. Only I feel so tired, I can't even be bothered to do it properly. Anthony looks at me expectantly. I always have some new idea of how to decorate the tree: silver and blue one year, or red and green the next. But this year I have no interest in a colour scheme.

'What shall I do?' he asks, waiting for instructions.

I shrug. 'Dunno. Put them all on, I guess.'

He frowns, puzzled. 'What, all of them?'

'Yeah.'

'But they won't match. You always say they should match.'

'Well, not this year, OK? Just bung them all on.'

He raises his eyebrows. 'OK. Whatever you say, sir.'

As we attach wooden trinkets and glass baubles, I try to remember how I used to feel at Christmas. Where has the magic gone? The delightful anticipation, the gut-tingling butterflies? Why does Christmas suddenly feel like any other time of the year? Why isn't it special any more?

'You look sad.'

I am startled. 'Do I? Sorry. I was just thinking that Christmas isn't the same any more.'

'Isn't it?'

'No. Every year it gets less special.'

'You must be growing up,' Anthony tells me wisely. 'Everything gets less special when you grow up. That's what I've heard anyway.'

His serious face makes me giggle. 'Oh dear. Doesn't sound very optimistic, does it?'

'No,' he agrees. 'Best to die young, I think. Then you don't have all that disappointment.'

Dad comes in as we are shrieking with laughter. 'Ah, so that's why the tree isn't finished yet. You're having a laugh while there's work to be done!'

'Old man,' says Anthony under his breath and I start giggling again.

'I heard that,' says Dad.

When Mum comes in I feel a flash of resentment, but I feel guilty for spoiling Christmas, so I make an effort to be civil. 'Mum, did you want to put the star on the top?'

She looks surprised. 'Oh, are you sure? I know how you like to do it.'

'No, it's OK.' I am making a peace offering and she knows it. I always put the star on the tree – it's my job. I like to do it. It feels as though I am putting the finishing touch to my creation.

Mum takes the star from me and carefully places it on the top, winding the ribbon around the branch. 'There.

It looks lovely. I like the higgledy-piggledy theme.'

'Emily said to just put everything on,' says Anthony, reliable as ever.

Mum puts her arm around my shoulders and gives me a squeeze. 'It's great. Now, why don't you both come and help me to make mince pies?'

For a while, it almost seems as though life has returned to normal. I can pretend to myself that I am happy. I can even pretend that we are a happy family with no worries. We laugh and joke with each other. Dad says something daft and we all giggle. Mum tries to frown but doesn't quite manage it. It's all just as it used to be.

Except that under it all, under the laughter, the excitement and the togetherness, something dark and gloomy lurks in me. I know it doesn't lurk in the others – I can see it by their smiling faces and shiny eyes. This gloom, this darkness, is only in me. And it is *there*, all the time. Sometimes I can go for hours without realising it. But every now and then I catch myself – laughing at a joke, or feeling good about myself – and suddenly I remember.

Deep down, so deep inside I don't know where exactly, there is badness.

I don't know if it's always been there and I just never realised – or whether I have created it recently from all the mess at school. But it's there – something rotten at the core.

Christmas comes and goes. I can't believe I feel this way

about it – but there's nothing important about it any more. I get some really nice presents, but a week later I struggle to remember what they were. Mum and I are trying to be nice to each other, and it's working, at least on the surface. I think she really has forgiven me for the cinema trip. But I can't feel the same way about her any more. Every time she says something like 'being a teenager is hard' or 'of course, school results aren't all they're cracked up to be' I feel as though she's making a personal dig at me. I feel as though what she's really saying is 'you're being moody and spiteful, but I can excuse you because you're a teenager' and 'you'd better get all As for your GCSEs because otherwise you'll end up stacking shelves in Tesco.'

The good news is I haven't cut once.

The bad news is term starts again next week.

monsters do not exist

The night before school starts I am a mess. I think it's because of the uncertainty. I have no idea what to expect tomorrow. How will Lizzie and the others behave towards me? Will they still be ignoring me? What am I going to do if this lasts for the rest of the year? And – what Mum would see as far more important – how did I do in my mocks?

I lie on my bed and stare at the ceiling. I am supposed to be asleep, but I have never been more awake.

Without warning, a nameless terror creeps over me. It starts at the top of my head and slowly tingles its way down my body. By the time it reaches my toes, I can no longer move. I am paralysed.

This is how I used to feel when I was small. I used to think there was a monster under my bed. I would wake up in the night desperately needing the toilet, and not be able to get out of bed for fear something would grab my ankles.

Now, suddenly, even though I am fifteen and far more rational than I was at five, the same terror grips me. I know perfectly well there cannot be a monster under my bed – monsters don't exist. But still the fear grips me, and I cannot even cry out for help.

The fear is tomorrow.

The fear is school.

And whilst I know that monsters do not exist, school most certainly does. And so do Lizzie and Marianne and Maia and Yasmine.

They are the monsters now.

I am scarcely able to breathe. I stare fixedly at the ceiling.

And then a tiny voice in my head starts to call me. *Cut, cut, cut, cut*, it repeats.

You know it will make things better.

You need to go to sleep.

If you don't sleep, you will be too tired for school tomorrow.

If you are too tired for school, you won't be able to do the work.

If you can't do the work, everyone will laugh at you.

You will be letting yourself down.

You need to sleep.

Cutting will help you sleep.

The fear doesn't leave me, but now I have a focus, I know what to do. I get out of bed, my whole mind filled with the image of the blade under my bed. I hid it there two and a half weeks ago.

I peel back the edge of the carpet and pick out the blade. There is a small patch of discolouration on one end. I examine it closely. It looks like dirt. But I can't go and get another blade from the bathroom. Mum will start to notice her razors are going missing.

I must start to get my own.

But for now, it will have to do. I wipe it with a tissue to get the worst off. And then I use it.

The relief is instant and overpowering. I cut a little deeper than I mean to, and the blood trickles down my arm. I mop it up with tissues, tenderly. I must look after myself. I am not well.

With the relief comes exhaustion. It's two a.m. and at last I can go to sleep. Tomorrow I know I will feel stupid and ashamed.

Tonight I feel released.

Patrice has a black eye. 'It's not that bad, is it?' she asks anxiously.

'What happened?'

'I fell over and banged my eye on a kitchen cupboard.'

'Does it hurt?'

'Yeah, but not as much as it did. The bruises are going away, aren't they?'

Yes, if you can call black and yellow 'going away'. 'It doesn't look that bad,' I reassure her. 'You won't be able to see it at all in a few days.'

'I nearly didn't come to school,' she says. 'I can't bear people asking me questions.'

'Me neither.' The fresh scar on my upper arm stings slightly. The thought of someone seeing it, and asking me what it is, fills me with horror.

'How was your Christmas?'

I frown. 'It was OK, I guess. I dunno, Christmas just doesn't seem the same any more.'

'How do you mean?'

'Well, it used to be special, you know? Like – magical. I mean, when you were little, it was so exciting, wasn't it?'

A flicker of something crosses Patrice's face, but I can't read it. 'Yeah, I guess so.'

'Wasn't it exciting for you?'

'That's not quite the word I'd choose,' she says, looking down at her feet.

I wait, puzzled, but she doesn't say anything else.

A tiny suspicion about her black eye creeps into my mind. Did she really walk into a cupboard? I've seen enough documentaries about domestic violence to know it really happens, but somehow I can't really believe it. Surely I'd be able to tell, wouldn't I? Patrice would be unhappy all the time, wouldn't she?

The thought disappears as the bus reaches the school gates.

I'll never know how I managed to walk into the form room. I just kept putting one foot in front of the other. Mr Simmons looks up and says, 'Ah, Emily. Good Christmas?' I nod and smile.

Lizzie and Marianne are at their desks. Their conversation stops abruptly when they see me. They don't say anything, but I can feel their eyes on me as I go to my locker. There's a note sticking out of the gap in the door. It says 'IT'S NOT OVER YET' in capitals. I know who it's from. I don't bother to turn and look at them because I know that's what they want me to do. I shove the note into my bag with shaking fingers.

The teachers have had all of Christmas to mark the mocks. Now, first week back, they can hardly wait to humiliate us. 'I am disappointed with this class,' says Mr Joannou. 'I know you are capable of better.' He makes it sound as though we have disgraced the school. I know that I am one of the ones to blame. My grade will be embarrassingly bad. He walks around, handing back the papers. My throat fills with bile as he approaches my desk.

'Not bad,' he says, throwing the paper down.

There is a large 'A' in the top right-hand corner.

No, this isn't right. He must have given me someone else's paper. Impulsively, I pick it up.

'Mr Joannou, this isn't right. You must have given me someone else's paper.'

He turns. 'Isn't an A good enough for you, Emily? Check the name.'

The class laughs and my cheeks burn as I read the name at the top. It is my paper.

I don't understand.

It is the same in my other lessons. I get an A★ in Art. I get As in Eng Lang and History. I get Bs in the others, except for German, which is a C.

I don't know how to feel. The week passes in a mix-ture of surprises. I have done well in my mocks. Not, perhaps, as well as I should have, but certainly not as badly as I believed.

What is going on?

Have I lost my perceptions? How could I have been so certain that I did so badly? *Why didn't I fail them all?*

My parents are pleased with my results, although I can tell they expected more A★s, and Mum starts talking about getting me extra help in German.

By the time I reach the weekend, I have cut again. Twice. On Thursday I find a small tin in the gutter and I take it home and wash it out. Then I put my blade in the tin and keep it in my schoolbag. Friday is somehow easier to get through knowing I have the blade with me, just in case. I don't use it, but I know I won't leave home without it again.

I don't know what to think any more. I was so *sure* I'd failed my exams. Am I going mad?

And what is worse is that I don't know how to feel about the results themselves. I suppose I should be pleased with them – after all, I didn't do enough work to pass any of them. But at the same time, I know that I am capable of getting top marks in virtually every subject – my academic history shows that. Why couldn't I have just kept going? What happened to all that discipline?

I am cross with myself for not failing.

I am cross with myself for not doing better.

I must be crazy.

Then, on Saturday, one of my cuts becomes infected.

you have to tell someone

I guess I haven't been keeping the blade clean enough. Some dirt must have got into the cut. It's red and inflamed, and yellow pus starts to seep out of it. It really hurts too.

I bathe it in the bathroom, and search around for some antiseptic cream. The only tube we have is two years out of date, but I put some of it on anyway. Then I put a clean dressing on it. I have had to buy dressings from the chemist because they don't make plasters long enough. Dressings are awkward, especially high up your arm, because the tape comes unstuck really easily and they fall off. I have been tempted to cut my right arm recently, because I am running out of space above my left elbow, but I don't know how I would dress my right arm.

In one way I am slightly frightened by the infection, but in another way it gives me a warm, comforting feeling. I am looking after myself. I am taking care of my body. I like doing that. It tells me I am good at something, I am in control.

Patrice is away for several days after that first day back. I miss sitting next to her on the bus, and I wonder where she is. The longer she is away, the more I worry about her, until in the second week I finally pluck up courage to visit her. I know where she lives because she told me she hated living next to the chip shop.

A man opens the door, but he doesn't look old enough to be her father.

'Hi,' I say, suddenly feeling that I shouldn't have come. 'Is Patrice in?'

'Who are you?' he says.

'I'm Emily. From school? I brought her some home-work.' It's a lie, but I can't think of any other excuse. 'Is she here?'

He looks at me for a moment. He's well-built, he must work out. This must be her brother, I realise. He has the same springy hair as Patrice. Funny, I didn't know she had a brother. 'She's not here,' he says finally. 'You can leave the homework with me.' He holds out his hand.

'Oh,' I say. 'Um. Well, I can't really leave the work with you, I have to explain how to do it. You know what teachers are like – never explain things properly.'

I grin, but his eyes are cold. It startles me, and I start to babble.

'Never mind, I'm sure it won't matter, I can give it to her when she comes back. Is she coming back soon, do you know? Because she's got her mock results – I don't know how she did, but I'm sure she did fine . . .' I trail off.

'She'll be back tomorrow,' he says, and closes the door.

As I walk away, I look back at the house. On the first floor, a curtain twitches, and a face hurriedly dips out of sight. I am sure it's Patrice.

Why did he say she was out if she was in?

Patrice does come back to school the next day, but when I ask her about my visit, she is strangely evasive.

'Your brother said you were out, but I saw you at the window.'

'Oh,' she says, and shrugs. 'Maybe he was just mistaken.'

'Mistaken?' As I turn to look at her, I brush against her arm. She winces. 'What's the matter with your arm?' I say sharply.

'Nothing.'

I stare at her, and suddenly everything clicks into place. How could I not have seen it before? The bruises, the absences from school. The strange way her brother behaved when I came to visit. 'Oh Patrice,' I say. 'You have to tell someone.'

The look in her eyes brings me up short. I've never seen naked terror before. 'Tell someone what?' It's a whisper.

'About your brother,' I say, lowering my voice too. 'He's — he's beating you up, isn't he?'

She stares at me for so long I think she's frozen. 'What makes you think that?'

'Patrice, it's obvious. I just didn't realise before. You're hardly ever in school, you're covered in bruises. No one walks into cupboards as often as you do. That's why you won't talk to people. That's why he said you were out. What did he do to you?'

She has gone so white I am afraid she will faint, and tears are starting to trickle down her ghostly cheeks. 'I can't tell you,' she whispers. 'If I tell anyone he'll kill me.'

I pull up the sleeve of her jumper, ignoring her flinching. Her arm is black and purple from the wrist to the elbow, and there are clear fingermarks around her wrist. I feel sick. 'Oh God.'

She pulls the sleeve back down, casting fearful glances around. 'You see? I can't tell anyone. It's too dangerous. You mustn't tell anyone. Promise me you won't.'

'Does your mum know? Why is she letting this happen to you?'

'She can't do anything,' says Patrice. 'She used to stand up to him, but she can't any more. She drinks a lot so she doesn't have to face him. And she stays out of his way.'

'What about your Dad?'

'Don't have one. He left when I was four.'

'Patrice, this is abuse. No one is allowed to do this to you.'

'You don't understand!' She lowers her voice again. 'It's not so bad. I can cope. I'm all right.'

'You're not all right, you're –'

'Stay out of it, Emily! *Please*. Please, for my sake. You mustn't get involved; you don't know what he's like. The school sent someone round the other day. I had to lie to them because he was there. Afterwards he got really mad at me. He said by missing school I was drawing attention to myself. He said he'd make sure no one would see the bruises in future. Please. You must promise not to tell anyone. *Promise*.'

What can I say?

'All right. But you've got to promise *me* something. You must get some help. There are people out there who can help you. And your mum. Promise me you'll do something.'

'I can't. I tried before, and – he found out. It was horrible. I can't risk it again. Besides' – she tries to look hopeful – 'he said he wouldn't do it again.'

I raise my eyebrows.

'I know, he's said it before. But if I don't make him angry, he won't hit me. It's my fault most of the time. Anyway, I'm sixteen soon. Then I can move out.'

'Move where?'

'I don't know. I'll get a job and find a flat or something.'

An image flashes across my eyes: Patrice in a dingy flat, with rats and cockroaches under the fridge, eating baked beans out of a can. I shiver. Surely there must be a better way? 'You can live with us,' I say suddenly. 'Come and live with me and my family.' Even as the words are out of my mouth, I know it's impossible. My parents would never agree to it.

Patrice knows it too, and her face looks somehow older. She gives me a pitying smile. 'Thanks. It's nice of you, but you know it wouldn't work. I don't suppose your parents would be thrilled. And my brother would come to your house. You don't want that.'

No, I certainly don't want that. The thought of that tall, muscled man thumping on my parents' door and demanding to see Patrice fills me with dread.

I feel so helpless.

'Don't worry,' says Patrice. The colour has returned to her face. She pats my hand. 'I'll be OK. Honestly.'

Why is she reassuring me? It should be the other way around.

That night, I lie awake for hours. The house is quiet apart from the usual creaks and hums. I want to stay awake because I have to think, but even if I wanted to sleep, I couldn't. I don't sleep very well at all now.

Tonight I have to think about Patrice. I never imagined that I would know someone who was actually being abused by a member of her own family. I've watched programmes, read articles, which told me that statistically I must know someone in that situation, but somehow I can't reconcile this with what's happening to Patrice.

I wonder when it started.

I wonder how long she's been enduring the beatings.

I wonder how often she's hit.

I wonder how she can stand to live day after day in the same house as him.

And I wonder: why her?

My body aches in sympathy for her bruises. I can almost feel her pain. It engulfs me, and it hurts even more because she is my friend. I don't want her to hurt. No one should hurt, no one should be in pain. Patrice is a good person; she doesn't deserve this.

As I turn over in bed, I brush against the cut that was infected and wince. It healed over finally, but it took much longer than usual. I've learned my lesson, though. I bought two brand-new plastic boxes from Superdrug – one small, one a bit bigger – and I keep the small one in my schoolbag and the big one under my bed. I waited until Mum bought a bumper pack of disposable razors, and then I took two. I'm going to keep everything clean from now on.

Nobody hurts me – I do it to myself.

Why do I do this? What earthly reason have I to be unhappy with my life? I have a loving family; I am good at my studies. I have a bright future. I have some problems with friends, but doesn't everyone?

Patrice is being beaten, day after day, week after week. She has *reason* to be depressed. What reason do I have? Instead of my being there for her, she is reassuring me that things will be OK.

Everything is the wrong way round.

Why is the night so long?

no longer invisible

Maia speaks to me the next day. 'How are you doing?' she says as she passes.

I am so taken aback I cannot reply in time, and she disappears round the corner unanswered.

I look around – she can't have been speaking to me. But there is no one else in the corridor.

When I reach my locker I discover that someone has poured ink in through the vent and my books are ruined. My French textbook is beyond repair. I will be charged for a new one. I am so tired I can't even feel angry. I don't seem to feel anything strongly any more. There is just this tiredness.

'I didn't know,' whispers Maia in Maths. 'It wasn't me.'

I look round. She really is talking to me. Her eyes are fixed on mine, but when I meet her gaze, she looks away. 'Oh,' I say.

'It was Lizzie's idea,' she says to her book. 'I found out too late. I would never . . .'

'Quiet, please,' says Mrs Begum.

I do my Maths as usual, but inside there is a tiny glow. Maia doesn't hate me after all.

She speaks to me again at lunchtime, after first checking that Lizzie and Marianne are nowhere to be seen. 'I'm really sorry, Emily.'

'Oh,' I say. Why am I suddenly so inarticulate? 'Right.'

'I didn't realise it would go on so long. I've wanted to talk to you for ages. But Lizzie said if any of us spoke to you, we'd be out of the group.'

It sounds so pathetic, like being at primary school. But exclusion from a group is the most deadly threat – I should know.

'How've you been?' I ask, collecting my tray.

'Good,' says Maia. There's a pause. 'I missed you,' she adds finally.

I look at her in surprise. 'Thanks.'

We reach the end of the lunch line and she goes off to the usual table. I walk slowly in the other direction.

Things don't change overnight, but Maia speaking to me does make my life a little more bearable. I know I am no longer invisible.

One day there is a note in my locker from her. 'Meet me after school by back gate? V important. Maia.'

I am suspicious. What if it's a trick? What if Lizzie and Marianne have been encouraging her to speak to me so that I will trust her again and then they can play some horrible joke on me?

But what if it isn't? Maybe this could be my only chance to make friends with Maia again?

I go.

Maia is standing by the gate. She looks anxious. Her eyes are darting around, and she grabs my arm roughly as I reach her. 'Quick, let's go somewhere they won't see us.'

We head round the corner into a side road. 'What's the matter?'

She still has hold of my arm. 'I have to talk to you. I'm really scared.'

We go a little further down the road, out of view of the school.

Maia drops my arm at last. 'It's Lizzie. I don't think she likes me any more.'

I almost laugh, but I choke it back.

'She and Marianne and Yasmine have started going around without me. I can't work out if they're doing it on purpose or if it's just an accident. They all went out to the cinema without me last Thursday. When I asked them why they hadn't invited me, they just said they forgot. How can you forget something like that, Emily? Do you think they're freezing me out?'

I stare at her, momentarily dumbfounded.

'Please, Emily, you've got to help me. I don't know what I'll do if they get rid of me. I'm not strong like you, I'll fall apart. I need friends. I can't stand being on my own. What do you think I should do?'

I'm not strong like you. I'm not strong like you.

My mind is trying to grapple with this. Maia is asking me for help. She wants to prevent the same thing happening to her. But I can't just wipe out the past like that. I've endured two months of silence from her, and now she expects me to help?

But if it were the other way around? Would she help me? I doubt it.

I open my mouth to say all this, but I can't utter the words. She looks so desperate. I can't do to her what she did to me. I know how she feels.

'You have to get back in there,' I say firmly. 'Organise something yourself – something big, something special. Make them be grateful to you. That way, they'll let you back in. You mustn't go around pretending you haven't noticed.' *Like I did.* 'You mustn't confront them either.' *Like I did.* 'You have to make yourself so important to them that they don't want to freeze you out.'

'Do you think that'll work?'

I shrug. 'I don't know. It's all I can think of.'

She hesitates a moment and then throws her arms around me, crushing my left shoulder. I bite my lip to stop myself wincing. 'Oh God, thank you so much. You don't know how I feel – I've been going out of my mind. I thought I was going crazy. I always liked you, Emily. I know we were never really best friends, but I thought Lizzie was horrible to you.'

So were you, I think, but I can't bring myself to say it. I smile weakly as she releases me. My newly healed scar throbs.

'You won't tell anyone, will you?' she says anxiously.

I shake my head.

'I'll see you around,' calls Maia as she runs off.

I feel suddenly dizzy, and I put out my hand to catch

hold of the nearby low wall. A boy walking along the other side of the road looks at me curiously.

I pull myself together and set off back to the bus stop. I have missed my normal bus, so I have to wait fifteen minutes for the next one.

'You're back late,' says Mum.

'I missed the bus. You're back early.'

'I had to pick up Anthony.'

'Why? What's the matter?'

She sighs. 'He fell over in the playground and bashed his nose.'

'Fell over?'

'That's what he says.'

I go up to his room. 'Hi there.' He's under his duvet, a small shape huddled in the middle of the bed.

I sit on the edge of the bed. 'Rough day?'

'Yeah.' His voice is muffled by layers of bedding.

'Aren't you baking under there?'

He emerges, blinking. His face is flushed and his eyes shiny. Dried blood rims his nostrils.

'What happened?'

'You must promise not to tell Mum.'

It seems all I ever do is promise to keep other people's secrets these days. 'All right.' One more secret won't make any difference.

'Reis Hunter pushed me over.'

'Who's Reis Hunter?'

'He's in my class.'

'Why did he push you over?'

Anthony shrugs. 'Dunno. Think it's my turn.'

'What do you mean?'

'He shoves loads of people. He's always in trouble. He hit a teacher last term.'

'Why wasn't he expelled?'

'Don't know. Think his dad complained.'

'Typical. So why did he pick on you today?'

'I think I was just in the way.'

'Why don't you want to tell Mum?'

'What for? She'd only march down there to complain I'm being bullied or something. Then he really would pick on me. It probably won't happen again.'

Patrice has gone kind of quiet on me. I don't blame her. It must have been a shock when I figured out what was going on. I don't understand why her mum doesn't do anything, though. Surely she should protect her daughter? I can't imagine my mum letting anyone hurt me like that.

I shop for razorblades now. I didn't realise they were available in packets from the supermarket. Of course, I have to pretend I'm sixteen, because they wouldn't sell them to me otherwise, but this isn't difficult, because I nearly am sixteen anyway.

Sixteen.

How strange.

Things improve gradually at school. Or maybe it's just that I don't notice things so much any more. Maia is definitely speaking to me again. My advice about how to deal with Lizzie seems to have worked (how ironic!)

and she is so grateful she is happy to talk to me in any Lizzie-less classes. But somehow I can't summon up much enthusiasm about talking back. I can't forget how horrible she was to me. I know it wasn't her decision, but she could have said no. She could have told Lizzie and Marianne that she wasn't going to ignore me. But she didn't. And now she talks to me all through Art, which really irritates me since I like to work in silence. It's the only lesson in which it doesn't matter if you don't talk to anyone. Why can't she talk to me in French or Science? Or when we're doing groupwork or pair-work? That's when I need a friend. But Lizzie is in those lessons.

January seems so long. And so cold and dark. I am glad, though, because it means we have to wear long sleeves the whole time, even in PE. I have started to cut lower down my arms. I like the visual sensation: the inside of my left arm looks so pure and white, and the clean red line looks so vivid. It's art, in a way. Sometimes I wonder about cutting words into my skin. Words that would explain how I feel on the inside – there on the outside, for everyone to read. But the problem is I don't know which words.

And then something awful happens. Patrice finds out.

does it help?

We're on the bus as usual, when there's a jolt as a wheel bounces down a hole in the road. I fall onto Patrice and yelp.

'Are you OK?' she asks.

As it happens, I'm not. The jolt as my arm rubbed against Patrice has dislodged a dressing. I clutch my arm and clench my teeth. The stinging subsides. 'Yeah, I'm fine,' I say.

She stares at me curiously. 'What's going on?'

'Nothing, nothing.' I try to smile, but my arm really stings. I reach down to retrieve my bag, which has fallen over.

'What's that?'

There is blood on the white cuff of my shirt. I freeze. Patrice is looking horrified. What do I say? 'Oh, er, that's nothing, I just – scratched myself by accident today . . .'

Her mouth tightens. 'Don't be stupid. As if I'd believe that. You know my secret. What's yours?'

I desperately try to think of some excuse, but nothing comes to mind. I reach for the button on my cuff, but I simply cannot do it. I can't willingly show anyone my scars.

Patrice sees that I'm about to refuse. So she just reaches across, undoes the button for me and pulls up my sleeve.

My arm is marked with jagged and sharp red lines. The most recent one is bleeding slowly, pulled open by the dislodged dressing.

Patrice doesn't make a sound. She stares and stares, until I feel uncomfortable and pull my sleeve back down again. Then she looks out of the window.

'Well?' I snap. She should say something comforting, shouldn't she?

'Does it help?'

She says it so quietly I hardly hear her. 'What?'

'Does it – help? When you do that? Does it make things better?'

My eyes fill with tears for no reason. 'Yes. Sometimes.'

She nods. 'Yes, I can see that it might.'

We sit in silence for the rest of the journey.

That night I get out my blade as usual, but as I prepare my arm, I hesitate. I feel unnerved by the way Patrice reacted. I don't know why I should, because she has been through so much herself. But I expected her to be angry – to say, 'Why are you doing this to yourself?' She was so understanding and sympathetic. Why do I feel cross about it?

I find a gap on my arm and draw the blade across it.

The red line jumps to the surface. But nothing happens. I don't feel any different.

A slight feeling of panic grips me. Why isn't it working? I stare down at my arm, willing the relief and euphoria to flood through me. But nothing happens. I still feel angry, confused, despairing.

I haven't done it right. That must be it. Maybe I chose the wrong area. Or maybe I didn't cut deep enough.

I wipe away the blood quickly and try again, parallel to the first. It is a little deeper, and the blood swells enthusiastically.

I drop the blade to grab a tissue and press down on the cut. It is a little scary to see that much blood. It doesn't stop as quickly as I am used to. I have to use four tissues. After a couple of minutes, it slows.

But still nothing happens.

I lie back on my bed, clutching the tissue to my arm, and stare at the ceiling.

Why hasn't it worked? Why, why, why?

It's worked all the times before! Did I do something different? I mentally run through my routine of preparation and cleaning up.

No, it was all in the same order as usual.

So why do I still feel so bad?

Fear creeps up on me. What if – what if it won't work any more?

Oh my God. *What if it won't work any more?*

What am I going to do if I don't have this any more?

I stare at the ceiling with such intensity that I give myself a blinding headache.

I don't sleep at all that night. I lie awake, worrying . . .

The next day I feel numb. It is like my best friend just died. I can't believe it has stopped working. I can't concentrate on anything. I don't even notice that Patrice is beaming at me when she gets onto the bus.

'Thank you so much,' she whispers.

'What? What for?' I can hardly keep my eyes open.

She glances around, then pulls up her left sleeve. There is a four-inch cut running up the inside of her arm. It is not deep, but the edges have not knitted properly and it is still oozing slightly.

I feel as though I have been punched in the stomach. I can think of absolutely nothing to say. I am so angry. How dare she? How *dare* she take away the only thing that is mine, all mine?

'You were right,' she is whispering. 'It really helps. When I was scared last night, I did it. I just did it. With a kitchen knife. And it made everything go away. I felt so much better.'

I feel sick. I don't want to know what she used. I don't want to know why she did it. I am dizzy with the thought that it worked for her last night *and it didn't work for me*. Wild thoughts rush through my head. Maybe by simply telling her about it, I have destroyed its power. Maybe I transferred it to her somehow?

She is looking anxious now. 'What's the matter? I thought you'd understand.' She looks down at her arm. 'It looks fantastic, doesn't it?'

I stumble to my feet, even though we are not yet at

the school. I think I may actually be sick. I need some air. Her arm looks horrible. It's disfigured. How could she do that to herself?

'Emily?' Patrice follows me down the bus, worried. 'What is it? Why won't you talk to me?'

I reach the ill-fitting doors and take huge gulps of air, trying to ignore the interested stares from the other people on the bus. 'It's disgusting,' I hiss at her. 'I can't believe you did it.'

She looks totally bewildered. 'What? What do you mean? You do it.'

'Yes,' I almost spit at her. 'But I didn't think you'd be stupid enough to do it too.'

'I don't understand. It helps, you said. Well, it helps me too! Why shouldn't I use something that makes me feel better?'

The bus stops suddenly outside the school and I jump off. Patrice follows me like an annoying dog. 'It doesn't just have to be for you! Why can't I do it too? If it helps me?'

I turn on her and snarl, 'Piss off. Just – piss off. Leave me alone. I don't want to talk to you.'

Shock registers on her face and she stands still as I walk away.

It is three days later that Maia pulls me aside in Art. She is full of gossip.

'You know that girl Patrice?' she says, excitement almost brimming over.

I frown. 'Sort of. She goes on my bus.'

'Well,' Maia looks around and drops her voice, 'I was talking to Shannon. She's in Patrice's classes for most things. She said Patrice's arm is covered in cuts. Right up to the elbow. Shannon saw it in History because Patrice's sleeves were too short for her arms.'

I don't know what to say. I feel sick.

Maia is obviously puzzled by my reaction. 'Isn't that just the most disturbed thing you ever heard? Cutting your own arms? I mean, how messed up must *she* be? And just to do that to yourself –' She shudders. 'It makes me feel sick.'

'Me too,' I say, because it's true. I pull my cuffs down slightly.

'Anyway, Shannon said she was going to tell Miss Jarrow. I mean, Patrice could be *dangerous*. What if she decides to cut someone else's arms instead of her own? She shouldn't be allowed in school. Think of all the damage she could do in *Biology*, for God's sake. We're always using scalpels and things.'

Fortunately, Mrs Knowles notices we're talking and she tells Maia to get on with her work. I sit down in front of my canvas and stare at it without seeing it.

What would Maia say if she knew I cut myself too? I can picture her face, eagerly telling Yasmine and Lizzie. Would she say I was disturbed? Am I disturbed? Maybe I am. Maybe I'm actually going mad. How would I know?

Am I dangerous? Just hearing Maia say the word 'scalpel' makes me queasy. But that's because I know I would use it on myself. I wouldn't hurt anyone else with it.

Or would I?

I cannot draw anything in the rest of the lesson. When the bell rings, I go to the toilets and lock myself in a cubicle. I cannot possibly go to Maths.

I stare at the door. It used to be a sort of white shiny surface, but years of use have covered it in scratches and rubbed-in grime. There are the remains of a poster stuck on the inside, explaining what you should do with your sanitary towels and tampons. Someone has drawn stupid faces on the tampons, and someone else has written 'Mr Hicks', the name of the History teacher, next to it with an arrow.

I am so tired. I cannot even feel my body any more. I pull up my sleeve and stare at the lines on my arm. I do not feel anything about them. I do not feel happy, or angry, or disgusted, or sad. But my brain tells me I should feel something. Am I severing my emotions along with my veins? Maybe the more I cut the less I can feel. It used to be the other way round – that cutting helped me to deal with my feelings – but now those feelings are so very deep they are almost buried.

But surely that is a reason to continue? Feelings hurt you. I don't want to feel anything. If you feel happy, something bad is bound to come along and spoil it. If you are looking forward to something, it'll never turn out to be as good as you thought. And feeling bad is just – the bottom of the pit. There is no light; no hope.

If you don't feel anything then you can never be disappointed.

The bell rings. I look up with a start. A whole lesson has gone by without my even noticing.

Patrice does not sit next to me on the bus that afternoon. Her face is pale and she looks terribly worried. I am not surprised. If Miss Jarrow finds out, she'll be in real trouble. Why did the stupid cow sit with her arms on display in the lesson? I would never do that.

Maybe she wants people to notice. Maybe she's just doing it for attention.

How pathetic.

I wish you would talk to me

It is my birthday soon. I know this in the same way as I know, for example, that tomorrow is Wednesday. But I don't feel anything about it. Mum wants to take us out for a meal. She's asked me if I want a party, but without much hope.

'No thanks,' I say.

'What would you like to do to celebrate?' she asks, with a kind of desperation.

I shrug. 'Don't mind.'

She looks at me for a moment, and her mouth twitches with worry. 'The cinema? A meal out? The theatre?'

'Yeah, whatever.'

'Which one?'

I shrug again. 'I don't mind.' And I really don't. I can't make that kind of decision. It is too tiring. I don't have the energy. 'Whatever you think.'

'It's *your* birthday, Emily,' she says quietly. 'You should choose.'

'Well, I can't,' I snap. 'I really don't care. Why don't

149

you choose for me? That's what you've always done in the past, isn't it?'

I didn't mean to say that last bit. It just came out. But instead of snapping back at me, like I expect her to, her mouth trembles and her eyes fill.

'I wish you would talk to me!' she bursts out. Then she claps her hand over her mouth and hurries away.

In the end she takes us out for a meal, all four of us. The food looks and smells delicious, but every mouthful is such an effort. I can't eat more than half of what's on my plate, and when I refuse dessert, Dad looks at me anxiously. 'But you love profiteroles.'

I shake my head. 'No thanks.'

I am finding it hard to look my parents in the eye. There is so much concern in their faces that it hurts me to look, so I keep my eyes fixed on the table.

On the way home, Anthony says plaintively, 'Why aren't you happy any more, Emily?'

I cannot speak because my throat has filled with tears.

relief

When we get home, I cut four lines on the top of my left thigh. And it works. Thank Christ. I cry silently for two hours, between one a.m. and three a.m. The outburst of emotion is overwhelming.

sixteen

It is February now. I am sixteen. And yet, in some ways, I feel so old. Old and tired.

And sick of it all.

being erased

I am standing by my window staring at the garden. It is snowing, and the ground is disappearing fast. Soon there will be no green patches left. Everything will be white. A blank.

I know I should marvel at the beauty. I've always loved snow. Anthony and I used to build snowmen and snow-women. Mum and Dad used to lend us stuff from the dressing-up box and we would dress our snowpeople in old nighties, bits of curtain and silly hats. I remember it now, but it seems to be a long way away, as though it happened to someone else. I remember it from the outside looking in.

I run my fingers over the scars on my arm. I don't even have to look at them now, I know what each one looks like, feels like. I've learned them by heart. They are silvery, save those that are red-raw in their newness. It hurts inside to look at them, so I make new ones that hurt outside. It makes no sense. I make no sense.

The ground is totally covered now. Everything looks the same; there are no features to the landscape. Is that what I am like? All the bits I knew, all the green bits, the bits that told me who I am: all are covered with the blankness.

I am being erased.

Who would have thought it could happen so quickly? I have spent sixteen years trying to make my mark on this earth and now, in the space of four months, I am turning invisible. If I were to die now, what would be left? Would I leave a hole in the world? Or would it simply close up, like a wound? Heal itself and grow over the top.

I don't want to die.

But I don't want to live either. Not like this anyway.

What other way is there?

I drift through school. Sometimes I catch a few instructions here, a telling-off there, but nothing breaks through my blankness. I am cocooned in snow: chilling me from the heart but protecting me from real life. I do my homework most days. But I find it impossible to focus for long enough and I know I'm not doing it properly. Why should I? Nothing makes any difference.

Miss Collins calls me back after class.

'I'm worried about you, Emily,' she says. Then she waits.

I am not sure what I am supposed to say, so I shrug.

'Is everything all right at home?' she asks. Her voice is low and soothing, nothing like the voice she uses in class.

I stare at her from behind my wall of snow. How can

I answer? Of course everything is not all right at home. But that is only because *I* am there. When I am at school, everything is not all right here either. It is not the place, I want to tell her. It is the person. It is *me*. I am what is wrong.

But of course I can't tell her. And even if I could, what difference would it make? She would not understand. So I paint my face with my smile (I can still find it there sometimes, when I give my muscles a nudge) and say, 'Of course everything's all right, Miss Collins. I'm fine.'

She looks at me and for a moment I am terrified. It has not worked. Maybe I am using the wrong smile. It is such a long time since I have smiled properly that I'm not sure I can remember how to do it. Can she see right into me? But then she smiles back and I know she has believed my lie. 'You know you can always come and talk to me,' she says, and reaches out to touch me on the arm.

I jerk my arm back and cover the movement by picking up my schoolbag. 'Thanks, Miss Collins. I will.'

Another lie. I will never come to you, Miss Collins.

Of course, the time comes when my parents find out.

a total accident

I suppose deep down I had known that they would, but I have buried the fear so deep, kept it to myself for so long, that when the day finally comes, it is a terrible shock.

Mum and I are in the kitchen. It is after dinner, and Anthony has gone up to bed. I am emptying the dishwasher of its scalding load. Mum is getting chops out of the freezer for tomorrow night's dinner. She turns just as I reach for a large plate at the back, and my cuff slips up over my wrist. Several long scratches are suddenly revealed. It is a total accident.

She steps back, the breath catching in her throat. 'What are those?'

I freeze, holding the plate, which is burning my fingers. I can't speak. I can't even turn to look at her. Instead I stare at my wrist, at the collection of criss-crossing lines revealed in their nakedness, some white, some pinky-red. Two, from three days ago, still raw. I have no space left on my upper arm any more; I had to move further and further down towards my hand. I should have continued to cut my thigh. That would have remained hidden.

I put the plate down on the side and pull my cuff back down. But it is too late, far too late.

She steps forward and grabs my arm. Then she pushes the sleeve up. The friction against the new cuts makes them sting.

'Oh my God.' She has to clear her throat because the sound she makes is so croaky. She stares and stares at my arm. Then something in her snaps, and the frustration and anger at me boils over at last. Her voice goes up. 'What is going on? What are these, Emily? Oh my God,' she tugs and pushes at my jumper, 'they go all the way up your arm! What is happening, *what is this*?'

I still can't speak, but this is because my throat has closed up completely. I'm not even sure I can breathe. I try to twist away, but she is gripping my wrist. She looks frightened and angry. I suppose I should be worried that she looks like that, but somehow I don't feel anything.

'Well?' she says loudly. 'I'm waiting for an explanation.'

I stare at the floor. What can I say that would explain anything?

'Well, let's see what your father has to say about it,' she says finally, and drags me into the lounge.

Dad is sitting on the sofa watching the news. Mum picks up the remote with her free hand and switches it off.

'What's the matter?' he says, looking up. Mum thrusts my arm into his face. I nearly lose my balance.

'*This* is the matter. What do you make of this, eh?'

Dad stares at my scars. I wish I were anywhere but here. I'd even prefer to be at school. I try to remove my mind from my body, but the pain in my arm is tugging me back. Waves of nausea are breaking over me. I feel cold and shivery. Why doesn't he say something?

'Well?' snaps Mum.

Dad looks up at me. He suddenly looks like that painting of *The Scream*: white, lined and terrified. 'What – Emily – how did you get these?'

Tears are bubbling in my eyes from the throbbing in my arm. 'I –'

'Let go, for God's sake, Fran,' says Dad.

Mum lets go, and I pull my arm to my stomach, rubbing and cradling it like a baby.

'Sit down,' says Dad.

I don't want to, but I sit gingerly on the sofa. My body is in revolt. My cells are having a mutinous meeting, yelling and shouting, 'Get us out of here! We want out, we want out!' But my brain is overriding them: 'Now look, we have to sit and face this one out. It's just a storm, it'll blow over soon. I'll see you through, don't you worry.' And the voices in my head and the feelings of despair are starting to build like a gathering fog.

'Now, Emily,' says Dad quietly, 'I think you'd better tell us what's been going on.'

I stare hopelessly at the carpet.

'Is it someone at school?' asks Mum. She is trying to be controlled, but her voice is still too high.

I shake my head.

'What about that Lizzie? I never liked her.'

I shake my head again.

'Well, who is it?' Mum demands. 'Tell us, Em, you have to tell us.'

'It's no one,' someone says. I think it's me.

'No one?' Mum repeats. 'Then how did they get there?'

Dad suddenly breathes in through his nose. 'Oh God,' he says.

I know he knows. And actually, the fog starts to clear a bit. Because now – he knows. They will know. I know. You know. He/she/it knows. We know. You know. They know. And so the telling of them is done. I'll never have to tell them again. I am very tired.

'Are you – are you doing this to yourself, Emily?' he says.

I nod at the carpet.

Mum suddenly bursts into tears. 'Oh God,' she cries. 'Oh God, why, Emily? Oh God, as if it wasn't already bad enough what with Ant and . . .'

What is she talking about – 'what with Ant'? Ant hasn't got anything to do with this.

'I don't think I can cope,' she sobs.

She can't cope? The fog of emotion is rising again. It is no longer white and reassuring – it is black and red and filling my body with anger and hurt. It is starting to engulf me. I am disappearing from sight. Dad is reaching out for me but I shrink from him. My skin hurts all over. The thought of him touching me repels me.

Mum gets up and runs from the room, making a horrible moaning sound.

'Oh Emily, why couldn't you tell us?' says Dad from a long way away.

But I cannot answer him. For one thing, I don't know the answer. I am too far away for him to hear me, even if I were to shout. In my place in the fog, I hear Mum's voice echoing: 'As if it wasn't already bad enough, what with Ant and ...'

' ... what with Ant ...'

' ... what with Ant ...'

' ... what with Ant ...'

I frown. There is a meaning there, I'm sure of it, but it is slippery and wet, like a fish. It is something to do with Anthony and his learning difficulties, I think. And to do with Mum. *Think*, Emily! Why would Mum say, 'As if it wasn't already bad enough'? What is already bad? The meaning is within my grasp, I have it by the squirming tail ...

Anthony ...

Learning difficulties ...

Things being bad ...

Mum being upset ...

And then Dad blunders in with the stark, blinding explanation. Like a ray of sun scorching through the clouds.

'She'll be all right,' he says. 'It's just that we've never had to worry about you much. You've always just got on with things. She feels really guilty about Anthony, you see – thinks she should have noticed his problems

160

earlier. The teachers still aren't differentiating the work, so he still gets told off for not doing it. And they still haven't found a learning support assistant. It's been really hard for him, you know –'

'I KNOW!' I scream, so suddenly he actually jumps in shock. 'I *know* about his problems! I KNOW! How could I *not* know, living in this house? It's all you two ever go on about!'

'Em –'

'Nobody ever worries about *me*, do they? Oh no, it's always poor *Ant*, what a horrible time he's having! Can't do his homework, can he? Teachers being nasty to him, are they? Well, tough shit! He's not the only one having a shit time! Only I don't go on about it all the time, do I? No, I deal with it in my own way, in my own time! And it's none of your FUCKING BUSINESS!'

I leave the room. I have to do something very quickly, otherwise I'm going to explode. On the way up the stairs I'm already scratching as hard as I can at my scars. I want to rip the skin, shred it to pieces. I deserve it, after that outburst. I had no right to say those things. I never swear either. I don't know where that came from. They are disappointed and hurt by what I've done and said. I should feel the pain they're feeling. And after that, I shall be able to be calm again.

I reach my room and fumble with the handle. My body feels strange, like it doesn't belong to me any more. I'm not sure I could stop if I tried, but I don't want to stop. I need to cut – need it, like air, like water.

I reach for the box under my bed and take out my

blade. I need some more; this is my last one. As I pull tissues out of the box in readiness, I sit on the floor and stretch my arm out, resting it on my knees. I look at my arm – where to cut this time? There isn't much room left. Perhaps I should cut across my old scars. Like noughts and crosses. I pull up my skirt and look at my thigh. There is plenty of room there, but somehow it is the wrong place for this occasion. It must be my arm. I look more carefully and decide.

My mind is clear now I know what to do. The feelings of confusion are leaving and there is only the black despair. My hands no longer shake.

I position the blade carefully and press. The skin parts to let the blade in. I draw it across three old scars. It stings, but in a good way. I need it to hurt. The blood wells up and starts to run down my arm. It is beautiful, like a crimson sunset.

My breathing steadies. My heart slows.

I watch the blood, tipping my arm so that it doesn't drip onto the carpet. It runs right down to my hand, and if I turn my wrist round, it makes red bracelets. It's perfect.

When the blood slows slightly, I take a deep breath and pick up some of the tissues. I hate to mop it away. It is important. But I don't want to drip on the carpet, or on my clothes. I sit for a moment, relishing the slight after-tingle.

I clean myself up as best I can. My head feels cool, calm. The fog, or mist, or the million voices at once, recede.

Instead there is only peace.

I go to the bathroom and bathe my arm tenderly. Cutting high up my arm makes it difficult to submerge in water, so I just splash the blood away as best I can. The water makes the cut sting so I am as quick as possible. Then I stick a dressing over the top and pull my sleeve down.

All is right with the world again. Now I can cope.

I sit for a while on the side of the bath. Then I hear footsteps on the stairs. There is a knock at the door.

'Emily? Are you in there?' asks Dad. I don't know why he's asking. Of course I'm in here, who else would it be?

'Yes,' I say.

'Emily, we need to talk.'

Talk it through, sweet talk, happy talking talking, happy talk. No, Dad, we don't need to talk. Honestly.

I unlock the door. The look on his face hits me right in the guts. 'Dad, I'm tired,' I say.

He follows me into the bedroom. My box is still open on the bed, but luckily there's nothing in it any more. I wrapped the razor in tissues and threw it away. The bloodied tissues I flushed down the toilet. I will need to buy more razors tomorrow if I want to feel safe again.

Dad sits on my bed. I wish he wouldn't. It reminds me of being a little girl when he used to read me stories before I went to sleep. It feels wrong now. 'Emily, please talk to us. We just want what's best for you.'

Do they? They've always said that, but what does it

actually *mean*? What is 'best' for me, and how can they know? I can't even begin to find the words that might explain any of this. 'Where's Mum?'

He looks embarrassed. 'She's – er – she's crying downstairs.'

Great. Now I feel guilty about that too. Pile 'em on, Dad, keep 'em coming.

'Emily.' Dad looks up at me. 'Why have you been – doing that to yourself?'

Doing that. He can't even say it. I must be so disgusting to him. No normal person would *do this* to themselves. Maia's voice saying, 'I mean, how messed up must *she* be?' echoes through my head. I stare helplessly at the carpet. I cannot speak.

Eventually, Dad gives up and goes away. I only notice he's gone when I look up and he's not there any more.

I feel so heavy. I feel as though I weigh at least twenty stone. I cannot stand up under the weight any more, so I lie on my bed in my clothes and instantly sink into unconsciousness.

is it a sort of club thing?

It's funny, but I expected things to go on the same after they found out. I thought – what did I think? – I suppose I thought that once they knew, they would leave me alone.

Instead, the opposite is happening. I can't get away from Mum. She follows me everywhere, trying to talk to me. Two evenings later, she makes me sit down with her and Dad, and they cross-examine me. Mum looks dreadfully tired and the lines on her face have suddenly multiplied. But she leads the questioning.

Why am I doing this to myself?

Why can't I talk to them?

What is going on at school?

Where are my friends?

Has somebody put me up to this?

How the hell could I have thought this was a good idea?

Don't I know about the risk of infection?

And on and on and on. I answer when I can, but mostly I just don't know what to say. How can I possibly explain any of this when I don't understand myself? I can tell Mum is trying to be kind and understanding, but she is baffled and angry, and she knows that I know it.

'Did somebody else persuade you to start doing this?' asks Mum at some point. 'Is it a sort of club thing?'

I stare at her in astonishment. 'What? A *club?* What are you talking about?'

She says, 'Sometimes you have to do an initiation or something to belong to a club. Is that what you've been doing?'

I cannot even comprehend this. '*No.* No, of course not. I wouldn't be that stupid . . .'

There is a pause. 'So you know what you're doing is stupid,' says Mum.

I look helplessly at Dad, but he is somehow shrunken, and he won't look at me. His body language says he would rather be anywhere but here. It hurts so much to see it. My own father finds me revolting.

'I can't explain,' I say lamely. 'It helps me feel better.'

'*Helps you feel better?*' she says incredulously. 'In what world could cutting yourself possibly make things better?'

I wince. 'Don't call it that.'

'What? Cutting yourself? But that's what you're doing, Emily, isn't it?' She leans forward and glares at me. 'And it has to stop. Now. Right now. You understand?' She looks at my arms, which are carefully covered with a jumper. She starts to shake her head. 'Have you even thought about the permanent damage you're doing to yourself? What about the summer when you want to wear short sleeves? What are people going to think?'

I gaze at her sullenly. 'I don't care.'

'You will care when everyone you meet looks at your arms and wonders what's wrong with you.' Her voice is sharp.

I look at Dad again for help, but he is no longer there. I mean, his body is there, but his spirit has gone. He has withdrawn from me. He will no longer help me. I have driven away the only person who was always on my side. He sits there with a blank expression, not looking at me; not looking at anyone.

Mum hasn't finished. 'I can't believe you would do something like this. You've had a happy home life. You're good at school, you've always had lots of friends. Why on earth would you deliberately cut your own arms?'

I stare at the table again.

'We've always done the best we can for you, Emily,' Mum continues. 'We've been there for you. We've taken you to art lessons, supported you at school. How could you do this? *What more could we have done for you?*'

There is a long pause. It seems she has run out of things to say. I shrug in answer to her last question. Nothing, I think to myself. There is nothing more you could have done. You're right. I have absolutely no reason to be *doing this to myself*. I must be going crazy.

Or – and this is obviously what my mother thinks – I am a selfish child who is doing it for attention.

But how can I tell the difference?

In the days following the Scene, my mother ruthlessly pursues me. I am not allowed to be alone in my room.

Indeed, she has searched my room. Fortunately, I had guessed she might do this and had moved my restocked box of blades to the very back of the top shelf of books. It's impossible to find unless you know it's there.

Every time I go into my room, she is there in the doorway, wedging it open. 'You don't shut this door again, you understand?' She doesn't trust me any more, and that hurts.

She makes me do my homework downstairs now, and she stands over me. It is impossible to concentrate. The one person who might have been on my side no longer looks me in the eye. When I appeal to Dad for help, or to persuade him to get Mum off my back, he just shakes his head and looks at the floor. It's like he can't wait to get away from me.

Patrice has been suspended from school. At least, that's what everyone's saying. Miss Jarrow gave us a guilt trip in Assembly about looking out for each other. Being there for our friends and all that. I wonder what's going on. Has Patrice managed to get out of her house and away from her brother? What about Social Services – isn't that their job? But if Patrice is sixteen, then maybe they won't care about her.

'I heard that Patrice was being beaten up,' whispers Maia on the way out of Assembly. 'That's why she's been cutting herself. She's been abused. And she couldn't tell anyone about it because it was someone in her family.'

I marvel at the school grapevine. The communication here is faster than light. I don't bother to wonder how the news got out in the first place. There is no safe place to talk in this building. Someone will always hear you.

'Isn't that just the saddest thing?' murmurs Maia sympathetically. 'No wonder she's been – you know. She must have had nowhere else to turn.' She hurries off, shaking her head. Lizzie walks past with Marianne. They don't even notice me, and it's not deliberate. I have ceased to exist in their sphere of life.

Later, I get off at Patrice's stop and walk by her house. The curtains are drawn and there's no sign of anyone. Despite my cocoon of depression, I am worried about Patrice. I do hope she's all right.

When I get home, I go straight to my room. Mum has taken to coming home early from work. I think she's changed her hours so that I'm never alone in the house. But today she must have been held up. I have a few minutes to myself for once. A few precious minutes for a quick fix.

I reach up to the top shelf for my box.

It's not there.

My fingers scrabble on the empty wood, and I desperately reach along.

Where is it? I need it!

Relief. There is the box.

I take it down carefully, tenderly, and put it on the bed.

I sit down cross-legged and reach for the box of tissues. If I am quick, she need never know.

I open the box.

Then I stare in horror.

My blades have gone. Instead, there is a note: *I have removed the blades for your own safety*. It is unsigned, but I know the writing.

My mind goes blank.

How could she do this? How did she find them? She must have been going through my stuff!

It's like reading my diary or something. No, it's worse. She must have looked in every single nook and cranny of my room. She's touched everything in here. I have been invaded! I mean, I knew she'd searched my room before, but that was when I was here. This time, she's waited until I've gone out. She must have spent hours in here.

My breath quickens. I feel dizzy. I have to cut. Now.

I go into the bathroom, but the nail scissors have vanished.

I go downstairs to the kitchen, but I already know she will have removed all the kitchen knives.

I am right. There is nothing more dangerous than a fork in the drawer.

Desperately, I look around. What can I use? This is a kitchen, for God's sake; there must be something sharp in it!

My eye falls on the food processor.

Seconds later, I have dissected the processor and taken out the metal slicer. It is an odd shape and is much bigger than my usual blades. But it will have to do. I don't have much time.

I take the slicer upstairs with me and wedge my bedroom door shut. I can't possibly use this on my arm; it's too unwieldy.

I pull up my skirt. The lines on my thigh have started to fade now. Good, then I can make new ones.

I place tissues around my leg to catch the blood, and then I place the slicer over a suitable area and push.

It cuts cleanly, beautifully, but when I lift the blade away, I see the cut is much deeper than I intended. Blood springs to the skin and starts to pour over my leg.

I press tissues to my leg but it makes no difference. The blood simply soaks them in seconds. I run to the bathroom, trying not to drip everywhere, and grab a towel. I press it to my leg. Blood seeps around the edges.

Oh shit. Is it pulsing? Have I cut an artery?

The front door slams.

'Emily?' calls Mum. 'Are you home?'

I cannot speak. I want to cry out for help but I am terrified. I hear steps on the stairs.

She catches sight of me from the doorway. 'Emily, what —?' She looks down at my leg and her eyes widen. 'What have you done?'

'Mum,' I say in a voice that has no breath. 'Please — help. Help me.'

The next few minutes are a blur as she looks at the cut and tries to stop the bleeding. Then she bundles me out of the bathroom, down the stairs and straight into her car.

'Hold on, Emily. Just hold on.'

She drives like a maniac. I'm sure you're not supposed

to park right outside the hospital – it says 'Ambulance bays keep clear' – but she doesn't take any notice, and practically drags me out of the passenger seat and into the lobby. My leg is starting to throb, and I am feeling faint. How much blood have I lost? Am I going to die?

Mum is furious when they make her move the car. The triage nurse takes me into a cubicle and has a look at the cut. It's still bleeding but not as heavily. 'Right,' she says. 'That'll need stitching up.'

By this time, Mum is back from moving the car and is steaming with anger. 'Haven't you been treated yet?' she fumes.

'Don't worry, Mrs Bowyer,' says the nurse. 'Emily's going to be fine.' She makes me lie down and smiles at me. 'Let me just move this towel away. Ouch, that looks painful. It's almost stopped bleeding, though, and it looks like a clean cut. How did it happen?'

I glance at Mum, panicked. 'Er –'

'She fell against a sharp edge on the fridge,' says Mum quickly.

The nurse frowns, but she doesn't say anything. Then she cleans the cut with water and sees the other scars. She looks at Mum. Then she looks at me. 'Did you do this to yourself, Emily?'

I nod, dumbly. Mum makes a noise of annoyance. 'Does it matter? We're dealing with it. She won't be doing it again.' She glares at me.

The nurse glances from Mum to me and then back again. Then she fetches a small syringe and injects me with local anaesthetic. It stings. Slowly and carefully, she stitches up the cut with fine thread. She talks to me while she does it. 'There now, I'm just going to put a couple in at the top end. It's a little bit deeper there. It might be a good idea to have a tetanus shot, just to be on the safe side. Don't want you getting any infections, do we?'

I can't answer. Mum finds a chair and sits, glowering.

When the stitches are done, the nurse puts a padded dressing over the top and sticks it down firmly with tape. 'Now, you mustn't make any sudden movements,' she tells me. 'No running or jumping until it's healed. You'll have to come back in a week or so to have them taken out. I would have used butterfly stitches, but I don't think they'll hold it.' She looks at me seriously. 'Have you been doing this for a long time?'

I nod. 'But not on my leg.' It's really hard to say anything with Mum sitting there.

'Can we go now?' says Mum suddenly.

The nurse hesitates. 'I would prefer it if you stayed for a few moments longer. There is a psychiatric nurse on duty and I would like you to talk to her.'

'A psychiatric nurse?' says Mum. 'Whatever for?'

'Don't worry, Mrs Bowyer, it's simply procedure nowadays. Because Emily has been self-harming, we need to make sure she's getting the help she needs.'

Mum is speechless. 'Help? What help? We can deal with everything.'

The nurse is getting up. 'I'll let the nurse explain everything. Please don't worry.'

She leaves, pulling the curtain closed behind her.

I feel as though I have frozen. I can barely move from cold chills.

'I must ring your father,' says Mum. 'He'll be worried.'

I doubt it. She goes out without a backward glance.

I sit and stare at the sheets on the bed. And I finger the patch over the scar on my leg. It's only just been stitched up, but already I feel as though I'd like to rip the stitches out and let it bleed. I pick at the tape with my fingernails, but then Mum comes back in and I have to stop.

Mum and I sit in silence for what feels like ages. I wonder if I should say something, but I can't think of anything.

After what feels like an eternity, the curtain is drawn back and a nurse sticks her head in.

'Emily Bowyer?' she asks. I nod. She's younger than the other one. She smiles at me and steps into the cubicle. 'I'm Sue. And you must be Emily's mother,' she says.

'Yes,' says Mum. 'And we want to know why we're still here.'

'OK,' says Sue, perching on the end of my bed. 'I can see that it might be confusing for you, and probably making you anxious. I am part of the Child and Adolescent Mental Health Team at this hospital. There's always one of us around in Accident and Emergency.'

'Why? What for?' Mum sounds like she's in shock; she wouldn't normally be this rude.

'There are guidelines we have to follow,' says Sue. 'If someone is brought in with self-inflicted injuries we have a duty to offer them help.'

Sounds reasonable to me. Mum relaxes slightly. 'I see. What sort of help?'

'Well, it depends on what sort of help they need. But I think I can work that out better by asking Emily herself.'

'I hope you have better luck than I have,' says Mum, sighing. 'She won't talk to me.'

'Emily,' says Sue, turning to look right at me. 'Can you tell me what's been going on?'

'Like what?'

'Well, let's start with school. Is everything all right at school?'

I shrug. 'Not really. Just a rough patch, that's all.'

'Can you tell me about it?'

I look at Mum.

'Would you like your mother to leave?' asks Sue.

Mum's face crumples. She looks like that injured dog we found last year.

'No,' I say, reluctantly. 'It's OK.'

'I'm sure she'll be as supportive as she can be,' says Sue. 'But neither of us can help you if we don't know what's wrong.'

I pick at the sheet.

'Let's start with simple questions, shall we? What don't you like about school at the moment? Things or people?'

I bite my lip. 'People.'

'Staff or pupils?'

'Pupils.'

'Friends or not-friends?'

'Er. Both.'

'Can you explain what you mean?'

'Well,' I say. 'It's silly really . . . I mean, it's not important.' I just want to get out of here.

'Emily, anything that makes you unhappy is important. And if you tell me a bit about it, then maybe you won't feel so alone.'

I look up in shock. She nods. 'I can see that you do feel alone, Emily. Can you tell me about it?'

And strangely, I do tell her. Well, not all of it, but some of it. She nods. 'So the people you thought were your friends are making life very difficult for you.'

'I didn't know any of this,' Mum says. 'Why didn't you tell me?'

I shrug.

'Aren't you about the right age for GCSEs too?' asks Sue.

I nod.

'Are you worried about them?'

'Yes. There's too much work. I can't do it all.'

'Of course you can,' says Mum. 'It's just a question of getting organised.'

Sue glances at her for a moment. 'And what about home?' she says. 'How are things there?'

There is no way I'm going to tell her anything about home with Mum sitting there. School, maybe. But not home. 'They're all right.'

'No, they're not,' says Mum suddenly. 'How can you say things are all right?'

'Mrs Bowyer?'

'We found out about this – self-harming thing, and we just don't know what to do. My husband is no help whatsoever. He leaves everything to me. Emily won't talk to me, and we have a son who's been diagnosed with learning difficulties. I just don't know what to do. This –' she waves a hand at my leg '– is totally beyond me. I don't understand it at all.'

'That's why we're here,' says Sue. 'To get help for you all.'

'I don't need help,' says Mum. 'She's the one who's been carving up her arms and legs.'

I wince.

'But it is making you feel stressed,' points out Sue. 'So we need to make sure that you are supported, so that you know how to deal with Emily's self-harming.'

'I know how to deal with it,' says Mum grimly. 'She just has to stop doing it. Problem solved.'

'I'm afraid it's not that simple,' says Sue. 'Self-harming can be quite addictive. It gives you a rush.'

Mum looks disbelieving.

'It can be as hard to give up self-harming as it is to stop smoking,' says Sue.

'Mind over matter, that's all,' says Mum. 'You just have to be strong about it.'

Sue smiles, but she turns back to me. 'How long have you been self-harming, Emily? And by that, I mean doing anything that deliberately hurts yourself.'

I open my mouth to say last November, but I remember the pinching. I've been doing that for years. And I used to hit my wrists against the bed frame when I was younger. Does that count? 'I don't know,' I say finally.

'Have you been using blades for long?'

'Since November.'

Mum catches her breath. '*November*?'

'Are you sleeping all right?' asks Sue, ignoring Mum.

'Not very well,' I say. 'It takes me ages to go to sleep.'

'Is that because you're thinking about lots of things?'

'I guess so.'

'Are you eating properly?'

'She always eats properly,' interrupts Mum. 'None of this microwave stuff at our house. Meat and two veg every night.'

I nod.

Sue looks at me closely. 'You are eating it? And keeping it down?'

'Keeping it down?' says Mum. 'What are you — are you saying my daughter is anorexic?'

'Anorexia is a self-harming behaviour,' says Sue patiently. 'And it is also an illness. It's nothing to be ashamed of.'

'I'm not throwing up,' I say firmly.

Sue nods. 'Good. Are you losing weight, do you know?'

'Don't think so.'

'And how do you feel, most of the time?'

My eyes fill with tears. 'Tired. Really tired.'

'Anything else?'

It's difficult to talk suddenly. My voice comes out all wobbly. 'I just wish things weren't so — hard.'

'What do you find hard?'

I shrug. 'Everything. Getting up. Going to school. Talking to people. I just wish I didn't have to do any of it.'

Mum is silent for once. I daren't look at her. Not that I can really see anyway, because everything is blurry with tears.

'Do you go out much?'

'Not any more. My friends won't invite me.'

'Do you have a boyfriend?'

'No!'

'And what did you used to do when you went out with your friends? Did you drink?'

'A bit. Not really. I always had to stay sober to make sure everyone else was OK.'

Sue smiles. 'How very sensible of you. Now, this may sound like a silly question, but I'd like to know. Have you ever tried drugs?'

'No.'

'Sure?'

I nod.

'And how do you feel about life in general?'

'Fed up with it,' I say, and start to cry properly.

'Have you ever thought about suicide?'

I frown and shake my head. 'I've thought about – about running away.'

'Running away? But not trying to end it all?'

I shake my head. 'No. But I sometimes wish it – would happen anyway. Without my having to do any-thing. Does that – make sense?'

Sue nods. 'It does.' She pulls some tissues from her pocket and offers them to me. I wipe my face and blow my nose, but it doesn't stop the tears. It feels like some sort of floodgate has opened – they simply stream down my face with no way of stopping.

Mum has gone very quiet. Sue turns to her. 'I think Emily is very depressed.'

'We all have our off days,' says Mum shakily.

'No, I mean clinically depressed,' says Sue. 'I mean she has depression.'

'But she's only sixteen.'

'It's not an adult-only illness. Children can have it too.'

An illness. I have an illness. Thank God.

'Can you give her something?'

'I don't think anti-depressants are the way to go with Emily,' says Sue. 'What I would suggest is some counselling. Perhaps for all of you – so that you can see how best to help Emily.'

'Counselling?' Mum shakes her head. 'I don't think my husband would come.'

'Well, perhaps Emily could see someone on her own to start with.'

There is a pause. 'What about school?' says Mum. I might have known she would get round to the GCSEs at some point.

'We can contact the school guidance counsellor if you like,' says Sue.

I look up in horror. 'No!'

'It's all confidential,' says Sue reassuringly, but I know

this isn't true. Everyone knows which kids see the school counsellor. They miss odd lessons, and they get to go to the Unit at lunchtime instead of going outside. I can't believe Sue thinks no one would know. 'The guidance counsellor would help you with getting through the school day.'

'I can get through it,' I say desperately. 'Please don't contact them.'

'All right,' says Sue at last. 'Not to start with anyway.' She looks at me kindly. 'Is there anything else you want to tell me, Emily?'

I shake my head. I am so tired again. I can't even think, I'm so tired.

'I need to take her home,' says Mum.

'Yes,' says Sue, getting up. 'I think that would be a good idea. You left your details with the front desk when you came in, didn't you?'

Mum nods.

'Then we will be calling you soon with some suggestions of how to proceed.' She smiles at me again. 'It was nice to meet you, Emily. And we're going to get you some help now. You're not alone.'

she's just gone off the
rails a bit

When the CAMHT finally rings, my mum doesn't even tell me about it. I am going to bed, limping slightly. But the door at the bottom of the stairs is open and I can hear Mum and Dad's voices. I don't know what makes me think they might be talking about me, but I stop and listen.

'They said she's on a waiting list,' Mum says.

'A waiting list? For what?'

'For the counselling.' Mum sighs. 'Can't you pay attention? I already told you that. She's got to have counselling.'

There is a silence. I can imagine Dad's face, puzzled, trying to work out what the right response is. 'Counselling?' he says at last. Well done, Dad.

'Oh, for goodness' sake, Geoff,' Mum snaps. 'Can't you at least show some interest in your daughter's well-being? She's depressed. She needs help. We all need help.'

'She needs to pull herself together, that's what she needs,' Dad says suddenly. 'She's just gone off the rails a bit. She'll be all right in a little while. We should take her

182

out or something. Buy her a present.'

I can almost hear my mum's incredulity. '*Buy her a present?* You – how can you even *think* that is going to help? She's cutting herself, Geoff. *Cutting* herself. With knives and razor blades, and God knows what else.'

'I thought you'd taken all of those away.'

'I did! But she's going to find something somewhere, isn't she? You can't go through life without finding sharp things. And even if she can't cut herself, who's to say she won't burn herself with matches or scald herself with hot water?'

'She wouldn't do that,' says Dad lamely.

'I don't know what to do, Geoff!' Mum wails. 'I don't know what to do! It's like being with my mother all over again! She wouldn't ever talk to me either – just locked herself away inside her own head. And you're no help. You and Emily used to be so close – now you can barely look at her! How do you think that makes me feel?'

How does it make *her* feel? What an insensitive cow! I sit down on the top step and hug myself to keep warm.

'You've left it all to me to deal with this!' Mum continues. 'And I can't do it on my own. You're her father. You're a part of this family. You can't just withdraw from the difficult parts.'

I hear a door slam. Dad has left the room.

I sit on the step for a while. I feel so tired again. Why is everything I do wrong? Now I am even destroying my own family. My family unit that has been so strong for so many years. They are falling apart because of me.

Anthony's door opens. 'Emily? Why are you sitting on the stairs?'

I shrug.

'Was that Mum and Dad arguing?'

'Yeah,' I say. 'But I think everything's OK now.' There's no point telling him the truth.

He comes to sit next to me on the step. 'Guess what? Mr Copley says there's a new teacher coming next week. Just for me.' He beams.

'That's great news. So they've finally found someone.'

He nods. 'Mr Copley says she's called Miss Sayid and she's really nice. She's going to come to English and Maths and History and French with me.'

'What about the other subjects?'

'They're not so bad. I do OK. Besides, if I get help in some subjects, then it might help me do better in the others too. I could think about them better.'

I squeeze his hand. Sometimes my brother is so much more intelligent than we give him credit for.

Mum mentions the counselling to me the next day. She and Dad are hardly talking.

'The Mental Health Team rang yesterday,' she says, as though it's the most natural thing in the world.

'Oh?'

'They've put you on the waiting list for counselling.'

'Oh.'

She sighs. 'The waiting list is about three months at the moment.'

My mouth opens to say 'oh' again, but she carries on.

'Three months is an awfully long time, Emily. It's already February. You've got exams in June.'

I flick an angry glance at her. I should have known she was going to mention the GCSEs.

'Don't get mad at me, I'm just saying it'll be a difficult time for you anyway. Starting counselling around then might be very hard.'

'So?'

She looks at me seriously. 'I was thinking we could go private.'

I don't understand.

'We'd have to pay, of course, but we can afford it. And it would mean that you would be seen very much more quickly. Within a couple of weeks, possibly.'

A couple of weeks? An icy feeling creeps over me. This is all moving too fast. I don't think I'm ready to talk to a counsellor. What would I say? What would they expect me to do?

'I don't want to,' I say.

'What?'

'I don't want to talk to anyone.'

'Emily . . .'

'No, you're not listening to me – you never listen to me! You're doing it again! You didn't ask me about this – nobody asked me. Why are you always making decisions for me?'

'Because you're obviously not capable of making them on your own,' Mum snaps back sharply.

The breath catches in my throat.

'You have taken matters into your own hands for

long enough, Emily. We don't know how to help you. I don't understand why you're doing this. You have to stop doing it. A counsellor will help you stop.'

'I don't want to stop!' I cry. 'I can't stop, I don't want to – you can't make me stop! I need it, you don't understand.'

I can't bear to say any more. It feels like I've already told her too much. I walk away, but I hear her say:

'Well, you can talk to someone who *will* understand. If you won't talk to us, you'll talk to them.'

I won't, I think as I bury my head in the duvet. I won't talk to anyone! All right, they can probably force me to go, but they can't force me to say anything. I shall sit there in silence. That'll serve her right for making decisions for me again!

I am in detention this week. Mum doesn't know yet but the school has sent a letter to say I will be late home on Thursday. It's because I haven't handed in any homework.

I don't know what has happened to me. I look back at myself a year ago, and I can barely recognise that person. I used to be happy, chatty, surrounded by lots of friends, top of the class. Now I am none of those things. It somehow feels as though that time was another life. I have detached myself from my old self. But what have I replaced it with? Who am I now?

I don't know what to think any more, how to feel, how to talk to people. I don't even know how to have a normal conversation. It used to come naturally; now I have to make a huge effort to work out how to talk. Listen to the other person, think about what they've said, think of my own reply, say it. It's all too complicated.

I don't want to stop cutting, though. It's all I know now – it's familiar, comforting. It keeps me going.

If I stop, what will be left?

Mum finds it hard to get me a counsellor. I hear her on the phone one evening, and she sounds annoyed. 'What do you mean, you won't see her because she self-harms? You're a psychologist, it's your job!' A pause. 'So you mean that even though she has been referred to counselling, and even though she desperately needs help, you won't see her?' Pause. 'Fine. I'll try someone else.' She bangs the phone down, then turns and sees me.

'Oh Emily.' She tries to smile but she looks exhausted. 'Trust you to have a difficult problem, eh? That one wouldn't see you because she has "no experience with teenage self-harmers". Surely counselling is counselling? But no, it seems not.'

My mouth twists.

'Oh, I didn't mean it like that.' She comes over, but doesn't seem to know whether to hug me or not. 'Don't you worry, we'll find someone. We just want to help you, you know. If I could make things better I would. You know I would.'

My eyes fill suddenly and I nod. She reaches out for me, but again she can't seem to bring herself to hug me.

I wish she would.

'Make what better?' asks Anthony from the doorway.

I wipe my eyes quickly. 'Nothing.'

'Emily's having a bit of a bad time,' says Mum.

'Again?' says Ant.

It's funny, but Mum doesn't react at all in the way I expect when she gets the detention letter.

'Oh dear,' she says. 'Well, I guess it was bound to happen. Never mind, eh?'

Mothers are so weird sometimes.

A counsellor is finally found, but it's a man. And it's a psychotherapist, not a psychologist or a psychiatrist. Apparently that makes a difference, although I don't know why.

'I don't want to see him,' I say when Mum tells me.

Her lips tighten and I know she's annoyed with me. 'Now look, I've been trying for days to find someone who can see you. The least you could do is go along and try him out.'

'Can't I see a female counsellor?'

She breathes in loudly. 'Yes, Emily, if you can find one who will (a) be able to fit you in before next Christmas and (b) know how to deal with a teenage self-harmer.'

'I didn't ask you to do all this.'

'That's not the point. You know you need help. David Reed is the only one I've spoken to who can see you so soon. And he has counselled girls your age before.'

So now I'm a category. Girls my age . . .

'Fine,' I say huffily. 'But don't expect me to say anything to him.'

'Fine,' she says. 'Then don't expect to get better.'

so tired

I don't know what I expected but it wasn't this. The psychotherapist's office is more like a sitting room than an office. There's no couch – well, there's a sofa but it looks rather too short to lie down on. There are two or three other comfortable-looking chairs and a low coffee table with a box of tissues on it and a jug of water.

David Reed isn't quite what I expected either. He's not very tall, and has masses of blond curly hair. He smiles at me. 'Hello, Emily. It's nice to meet you. Would you like to sit down?'

He doesn't indicate which chair he wants me to sit in and I hesitate. 'Where?'

'Anywhere you like.'

I sit in a chair by the window and twist my fingers together. The chair is too squashy for my liking. I try to sit on the edge of it so I don't sink down too far.

David Reed sits down in a chair to my left. 'Now, let's get the formalities out the way. Do you like being called Emily, or do you shorten it?'

'Emily's fine.'

'Good.'

I wonder what I'm supposed to call him. Is he a doctor? 'David' seems a bit informal. Mr Reed perhaps? But somehow I can't bring myself to ask. Maybe I can avoid having to call him anything. Maybe I can even avoid looking at him. This feels so strange. I look at my hands.

'Why do you think you're here today, Emily?'

I frown. Doesn't he know why I'm here? Why is he asking such a stupid question? 'Because my parents are worried about me.'

'And was it your parents who wanted you to do this, or did you want to?'

No, I did not want to. This is a stupid idea, coming to see you. I don't even like you. I don't know you. How is this supposed to help? I shrug. 'Don't care really.'

He nods. There is a pause.

Am I supposed to say something? What should I say? I clamp my hands together and hope that he says something soon.

But he doesn't. This is awful.

'I don't see how this is supposed to help,' I say suddenly. 'I feel weird being here. This is just – weird.'

'Does it feel weird being asked to talk to someone you don't know?'

'Yes.'

'How does it feel weird?'

I frown again. 'I just – how are you supposed to help when you don't know anything about me? It doesn't make any sense.' I close my eyes. It's all too much effort.

'You seem very tired.'

'I am.'

'What are you tired of?'

I shrug. 'Everything.'

There is another long pause.

'I'm tired of me,' I say, without even thinking about it. 'I'm tired of being me. I'm tired of my life. I'm tired of people getting at me all the time. I don't want to be me any more. It's too hard.'

A siren rushes past the window. I've always wondered why the pitch of the noise changes as the ambulance goes past.

'You're tired of being you,' David says. 'Who would you like to be?'

I had planned on not saying anything. How did I start talking?

'If you could be anyone and be anywhere, who and where would you be?' David asks again.

My legs are beginning to ache from being clamped against the side of the chair. I look at the carpet. Maybe if I don't answer, he'll ask me something else.

But there is nothing but silence.

I know I will have to answer. This silence is driving me mad. 'I would like to be a painter by the sea,' I say. It sounds stupid, even to my ears. I expect him to laugh.

'By the sea. What do you like about the sea?'

I don't know. I've always liked the sea. 'It's just − there,' I say lamely. 'It's interesting. It's moody.'

'Moody.'

'Yes. It's always changing. It's always different, every

time you look at it. But it doesn't – ask you things. It's just – there.'

There is another pause.

'I could look at the sea for hours,' I add. 'I like it when it's angry and the big waves are crashing.' God, I sound like a five-year-old.

'But it's not angry with you,' he says.

'No, of course not.' What a strange thing to say.

'It doesn't – get at you.'

'No. It doesn't need to. It's bigger than that. It's just – pure. Anger or calm . . .'

'So you would live by the sea,' he says.

'Yes. By myself. And not be surrounded by stupid people asking me stupid questions.'

'All by yourself.'

'Maybe I'd have a dog,' I say, surprising myself. Where did that come from?

'And the dog wouldn't ask you stupid questions, or get at you.'

I shake my head.

'And the sea wouldn't get at you either.'

'No.'

'Can you tell me a little bit more about people who get at you?'

'My mum,' I say with some force.

He waits.

I really don't want to talk about my mum. Or do I?

Actually, it would be really good to complain about her. I can't complain to anyone else. 'You won't tell her what I say?'

'Emily, counselling sessions are confidential. The only reason I would have to tell anyone else what you say is if I think you are at risk. Then I might need to tell someone else to make sure you're kept safe.'

'Kept safe? You mean, if I say I'm going to kill myself or something?' I say bluntly.

He grins. 'Basically, yes.'

'So you won't tell my mother what I say about her?'

'No.'

'All right.'

'How does your mum get at you?'

'She won't leave me alone,' I say. 'She's always asking me what I'm doing, checking up on me. She won't – she doesn't let me *be*.'

'Can you give me an example?'

Every day is an example. 'When I'm at home – if I'm in my room – she's always popping in and out. It doesn't matter what I'm doing – I could be reading a book, or doing my homework, or – she's just always in and out. Do you want a cup of tea, how's it going, did you know there's a programme on tonight about Shakespeare, have you got any spare mugs for washing in here, Ant says he can't find his ruler – I don't care! Why can't she just leave me *alone*?'

I am so tired again. I slump slightly in the chair.

'Does it make you tired to talk about her?'

'She makes me tired. Thinking about her, trying to work out what to say, what to do, makes me tired. I can never be good enough. It's too much.'

'Never be good enough? For whom? For your mother?'

But this is too difficult a question, and anyway I don't know the answer. Yes, of course, for Mum. But also for me. I can never be good enough for me. That's what I've always been told. You must do yourself justice. Don't let yourself down.

I shrug. 'Don't know.'

There is another long pause, but I don't care any more. Why should I fill the space? He's the counsellor, it's his job to talk.

'How did it go?' asks Mum, when I get into the car.

I shrug. I just want to sleep. 'All right.'

'Is he nice?'

I shrug again. 'I guess.'

'What did you talk about?'

I frown. 'All sorts.'

'Are you going to go back and talk to him again?'

'What's with the questions? Just leave it!'

She drives home in silence, lips pressed together again.

I go straight to bed when I get in and curl up under the duvet, fully clothed. David's last words play in my head: 'I would like you to come and see me again, if you would be happy with that.' Would I? Would I be happy? What does that mean? Does he think he can cure me? Do I need curing?

I didn't even mention my cutting. He knows that's why I'm there. Why didn't he ask me?

is she going mental?

'What is going on?' demands Anthony one day over dinner. 'What's the matter with Emily? Why's everyone being so quiet? And why won't anyone tell me anything?'

I keep my eyes fixed on my plate, but I can feel Mum's gaze flicking over to me. She doesn't bother to appeal to Dad for help; she knows she won't get it.

'All right,' she sighs. I look up in alarm. What's she going to tell him? I don't want Anthony to know about my arms. 'Ant, we're sorry, we should have told you, but it's complicated to explain. Emily is not very well at the moment.'

'She looks all right to me,' says Ant, staring hard at me.

'It's not the sort of unwell you can see on the surface,' says Mum. 'It's not like a cold or the measles. It's inside her, in her head.'

Ant's gaze returns to my head. 'Is she going mental?' he says.

I can't bear this. I put my knife and fork down and get up.

'Sit down,' says Dad suddenly. His voice is quiet but strong. He's giving me an order, but he won't even look at me. I glare at him for a moment. Then I sit down.

'I don't like you using language like that,' Mum tells Ant. 'It's not nice. And no, if you're asking if Emily is going crazy, she's not.'

How would you know? I think. You can't see inside my head. Sometimes I *feel* crazy!

'She's been unhappy for a little while,' says Mum, 'and now she's not sure how to stop being unhappy. It's called depression. Lots of people have it. My mother had it for a while.'

Grandma used to be depressed? I never knew that. But then she died when I was quite small, so maybe I just don't remember.

'So she's going to talk to someone who will help her feel happy again.'

'A school counsellor?'

'No, we've found someone outside. The school doesn't know at the moment.'

'And when she's been talking, then will everything be back to normal?' he says.

'Yes,' says Dad firmly. 'And we can forget this ever happened.'

Anthony nods, but I am staring at Dad in horror. What does he mean? That we'll all just wipe this 'nastiness' away? As if it had never happened? Has he *no* idea how I feel? That at the moment I cannot possibly see a future without cutting in it? That if someone took it away from me, I would surely die? How can he expect me to simply erase my whole being because it makes his life easier?

Mum notices my expression. 'I don't think it's as easy as that, Geoff,' she says.

I don't want her help. What does she know about it anyway?

Dad frowns at Mum. 'It's just a phase. A teenager thing. She'll grow out of it.'

I can't listen to any more. I get up again and leave the table.

'Emily,' calls Dad sternly. 'Emily, come back and finish your dinner.'

But I am done with listening to him. I go into my room and find my pencil sharpener.

I've done it before; I can do it again.

'How are you today, Emily?'

'All right.'

'How did you feel about last week's session?'

I shrug. 'OK. Except Mum kept asking me what we'd talked about.'

'Did you tell her?'

'No!'

'It's all right not to tell her.'

'But there again, you see, she won't leave me alone! It's got worse and worse. I mean, she always used to check up on me, but since – well, lately – she just won't let me be on my own. She's always trying to get me to spend time with her. I wish things could just go back to the way they were before.'

'How was it different before?'

'Well –' I start but I'm not sure how to go on. He waits. 'We always used to – the family – we'd talk a lot. You know, solve problems and stuff through talking about them. But they weren't always asking me questions. I just – I got on with things, you know? And if I was worried about something, or Ant was worried, we'd all sit down and talk about it and then it'd be, you know, sorted. And Mum just let me get on with things. I've always been – sensible. She knows – knew – she could trust me to get on with things. She didn't want to be inside my head. If I wanted to tell her something then I could, and if I didn't want to then I didn't have to.'

'So you feel that she wants to be inside your head?'

I nod.

'And when she comes into your room, it's a way of trying to get inside you.'

'Yes. And she's always asking me *why*. Why do I feel like this? How could I do this to them? Do what to them? I'm not doing anything to them! And she's always saying as if they didn't have enough problems already, with Anthony and everything. Well, that's not my fault. He's not – he shouldn't be – the only one allowed to have problems.' My voice trails away. This is a bit too personal for me. It's all right when I'm ranting about Mum, but this is different. The thought of admitting that I might have problems is too embarrassing. I shouldn't have problems; I'm the sensible, trustworthy one. Why should I think I have problems? There are people in the world dying from malnutrition!

'Do you feel that Anthony's problems are more

important than yours in their eyes?'

This is so exactly what I *do* feel that it's difficult to actually say anything. I nod. There is a pause. 'Well, not so much now. Now that they've found out – I mean, recently. But he's my little brother; he was always the one who needed looking after. I was – sensible. Responsible.' I realise that I'm sounding pompous. 'Well, I *was* responsible! I was doing fine! And it's not Anthony's fault. He's had a lot to deal with. He's got learning difficulties, you see.' David nods. 'And people were shouting at him all the time, and that just made everything worse because he couldn't think properly. And we all had to make sure he was OK, and I get that, you know? I mean, it's not his fault people don't understand him. I know Mum and Dad have been trying to help him. But it never occurred to them that I might – need some support too.'

'So Anthony needed a lot of help and support. And because of his problems, he took up all of the attention.'

I frown. 'I suppose. I hadn't really thought of it like that. Well, I kind of did, but . . . I like him. I get on really well with Anthony.' I am anxious that he probably thinks I hate my brother. And it's not like that at all, but I don't really know how to say it. 'He always needs looking after. That's all. And I try and look after him. And I try and be supportive for – Mum and everyone. My friends – well, my ex-friends – and I try and be nice and helpful all the time. And I'm just fed up with everyone else's problems! Why can't I have some for a change?'

'So you have always been a supportive person, even at school?'

'Yes. My friends were always ringing me up. "Oh Emily, I haven't done my homework, what am I going to do, my parents don't like my boyfriend, can I borrow your jeans, my nail varnish just chipped".'

'You have always been someone that other people could rely on – could turn to.'

'Yes. And I do quite like that. I like – helping people. I like being relied on. Well, I think I do. I just wish – I could rely on someone else sometimes. Not very often. Just sometimes.'

'What happens if you ask for support?'

'Well, I used to ring Lizzie sometimes. And I'd say, "Listen, I've got this thing and I want to know what you think." And she'd sort of listen for a bit, and then she'd say, "Oh, I don't know, Emily, you'll figure it out," and then she'd start talking about herself. And somehow we never got back to me.'

'Is Lizzie your closest friend?'

'Not any more. She was. We were friends for four years. There were other people in our group. But she was my best friend.'

'But you feel that she would make demands on you, and you couldn't make any demands on her, or ask her for help.'

'Yeah. I mean, we had a lot of good times. She was really funny, we had a good laugh. And I liked helping her out – I liked being the one she came to.'

'How did it make you feel when you could help Lizzie?'

'I felt good. Well, mostly,' I say, thinking of the holiday

assignment that she made me do with her at the last minute. Why didn't I say no? Was I a complete doormat?

David pauses, and then he changes tack. 'I wonder what you think caused things to change at school?'

Suddenly I feel really upset. Thinking about Lizzie had been quite nice – the fun we'd had, the jokes we'd shared. Now it's all gone. And I realise that I really miss her. 'Marianne,' I say bitterly. The word tastes unpleasant.

'Marianne.'

'She decided she wanted Lizzie to be her best friend. She took her away from me.'

'How did she do that?'

'She – I don't know. We were all such good friends to start with. Well, I always knew she didn't like me that much. She always seemed to look down her nose at me, I don't know why. But then – she turned Lizzie against me. And then she turned all of them against me, and they wouldn't talk to me. Nobody would talk to me. So I'd go to school and nobody would talk to me. And I'd come home, and Anthony would have had a really bad day, so nobody would talk to me there either because they were worried about Ant. And all the time, people keep telling me I'm supposed to be revising for my GCSE exams!'

'So everyone else seems to be more important than you are.'

My eyes fill. 'Yes.'

'But you've got problems too.'

It's hard to say it. 'Yes.'

bite the bullet and get on with it

After the February half-term, school piles on the pressure. My coursework is supposed to be in, but I haven't done the last essay for English, and I never finished my Geography project. Mr Simmons asks me to stay behind one day.

'Emily, I'm very concerned,' he says.

I try to look interested, even though I couldn't care less.

'You're very behind on your coursework. You do know the deadline is very close, don't you?'

I nod.

'It has to be finished otherwise you'll lose valuable marks. It could affect your overall grade.'

I nod again.

'Coursework is an essential part of many GCSE subjects. I see here you've got pieces missing from Geography, English and Maths.'

Maths? Did I have one to do for Maths? I can't even remember it.

'Oh,' I say. 'Yes.'

Mr Simmons puts his clipboard down and looks at me. Then he sighs. 'I don't know what's happened to you, Emily. You're a bright student. You could get straight As if you wanted to. Everything was going fine until this year. Now, I know you've had some problems with friends, but I understand that's behind you now.'

Yes, it's behind me. Now I have no friends. Much simpler.

'You were friends with Patrice too, weren't you?'

'Yes.'

He sighs again. 'I'm sure you must have been very worried about her. We all were. But she's getting some help now and she might be able to rejoin the school soon. I'm not sure she'll be able to take all the exams, but there's every likelihood that things will turn out OK for her.'

I nod.

'So now you just have to bite the bullet and get on with it, Emily. You haven't got long to go. Can't you just keep plugging away for the last few months?'

But a few months is such a long time.

I nod, miserably.

'Good.' He smiles. 'I know you can do it, Emily. It'll just take a final bit of effort, but you'll be pleased you did.'

'Why did Simmons want to see you?' asks Maia, catching me on the way out. She talks to me quite freely now, although Lizzie, Marianne and Yasmine never do. I don't know how she managed to avoid being frozen out of the group. Maybe they just don't care any more.

I shrug – I seem to shrug a lot these days. It's easier than talking. 'I got behind on my coursework.'

She looks surprised. 'You, behind?' She's not in half of my classes, so she wouldn't know about the times I've been told off in lessons recently. Or about the detention. 'Why have you got behind? That's not like you.'

'Isn't it?' I'm tired of this. 'What *is* like me, Maia? Perhaps you can tell me, because I'm really not sure myself any more.'

She gapes at me.

'Oh, never mind,' I say, walking away.

My life at the moment is like a series of short scenes. There must be other things that happen in my day, but I suppose they're so unimportant I don't remember them. Conversations with Mum, tellings-off from teachers, sessions with David – they all just seem to roll from one to the other, without having any effect on me. I still try to respond as I think I should, but I have given up expecting to get it right. Once, seeing a 'D' on a piece of schoolwork would have made me hide in shame. Now, it's such a regular occurrence I don't even catch my breath. It just makes me sink a little lower into myself.

The snow in my soul has gone, and I suppose it was never really there in the first place. I can't expect to cocoon myself from everything for ever. I still have to talk to people, smile, nod, respond, eat, sleep. I still have to drag myself through every day. I still have to cut myself in order to feel normal. But the effects of the cutting aren't as strong as they used to be. I have to cut more; cut deeper for it to give me that same over-whelming feeling of relief and peace. Both arms are now scarred from wrist to shoulder, and although I haven't dared cut my thigh again – it took so long to heal and to stop throbbing – I have tried to cut my stomach. It wasn't right, though, so I went back to my arms.

'I want to explore the idea of problems,' David says next time I see him. 'You said that you have problems too, like other people. We've talked a bit about Anthony. We've talked a bit about school and friends. I was won-dering what else you see as problems?'

God, he makes me sound like some whining idiot. I must be pathetic, not to be able to cope with basic day-to-day living. 'They're not really problems,' I say hastily. 'Not in the grand scheme of things. They're just little things really.'

'What sort of little things?'

'Exams,' I say, and almost laugh. 'I mean, everyone has to do them. I don't see why I should be getting in a state about them.'

'Are you in a state?'

I have to think about this. 'Yes and no. I can't seem to care any more. Everyone's told me so many times how important they are. I used to think so too. I mean, I guess I still think so. But I just can't do it. There's too much work.'

'Too much work.'

'Too many subjects, too much homework – I can't remember where I am any more! They all want me to do stuff, and I do it, but even when I do it I don't understand the point. I'm getting really bad marks at the moment in some subjects, and sometimes I mind – you know? Sometimes it bothers me, because I know it should bother me. I was always – good at school. Top of the class a lot.' I wonder if he thinks I'm boasting. I throw him a glance, but he just looks interested. 'But this year it's just all got too much. It's like some huge mountain I'm supposed to climb and I haven't got any rope.'

'That's an interesting comparison. It feels like climbing a mountain.'

'No matter how much work I seem to do, it's never enough. And so I don't really do very much now. I look at all the books and I don't know where to start. So I don't start at all. And it makes me worried.'

'So you do care about it?'

'Yes – no. Yes, I do care. Everyone expects me to do well, and I don't want to let them down. But it's too hard.'

'Does everyone else think you can cope?'

'Yes. Because I always have in the past. And I don't see why I shouldn't. Why can't I? I know how important these exams are. It's not as though I don't know! What with everyone telling me all the time! I can't get away from it – my teachers tell me I won't get a job without GCSEs, my parents say if I get less than an A I'll be letting myself down. I just – I wish it would all go away. Or that I could go away.'

'And be by the sea?'

That sounds nice. 'Yes.'

'With your dog.'

'Yes. And no stupid people.'

We sit in silence for a while. He leans forward slightly.

'But you can't go away. You can't go and live by the sea. So what do you do instead?'

I cut myself, I think.

But I still can't say it.

pain

I am still getting good grades in Art. It's about the only subject I'm likely to pass at this rate. Mrs Knowles is pleased with me. 'You've worked really hard,' she says. 'I am so pleased you've done yourself justice.' She is looking at my latest piece of coursework on 'pain'. 'This is a fantastic picture, Emily. You've really got right inside it to express what you want to say.'

Well, of course I have. It's on 'pain'. It's the one topic I know most about.

show us your arms, Emily

I am late to PE because one of my dressings has come unstuck while I changed. When I arrive, the class is jogging indoors because of the rain. We are to have volleyball in the sports hall.

Mr Holmes divides us into teams. I am paired with Lizzie, who barely gives me a second glance.

We have to wait for two games to be played before it's our turn. We don't exchange a single word.

Volleyball is hard work and we are all panting with exhaustion before long. I am very hot, but I cannot take off my sweater as I only have a T-shirt underneath.

'Come on, Emily!' shouts Mr Holmes. 'Move!'

I am dripping with sweat. Lizzie is not making it easy for me – mind you, we are both fairly crap at volleyball. But everyone else has stripped down to T-shirts and I am the only one still wearing a sweater.

'For God's sake, Emily, why don't you take your jumper off?' Lizzie snaps at me as I miss an easy pass. 'You look like you're overheating.'

I am. I'm starting to feel dizzy.

'Emily, you do have a T-shirt on underneath, don't you?' asks Mr Holmes.

I nod.

'Then why don't you take your jumper off?'

'I don't want to,' I mumble. He stares at me. So does Lizzie.

'What is *wrong* with you, Emily Bowyer?' she hisses. 'What the hell's the big deal about your jumper?'

Face scarlet, I shrug. 'Just don't want to take it off, that's all.' I am aching to pull my sleeves up, but I know I can't.

Lizzie stares at me scornfully, then turns away. We are about to lose the game anyway; I don't know why she cares.

In the crush to get out of the hall when the bell goes, I scrape my arm against the wall. 'Ow!'

Lizzie, squeezing past, looks at me for a moment. There is something odd in her glance, and it makes me feel uncomfortable.

Downstairs in the cloakroom, I take my shirt down from the peg. I have got really good at taking my T-shirt off and putting my school shirt on whilst wearing my PE jumper. There's a knack to it. Some of the other girls are shy, so it's not that unusual.

Lizzie, in her bra and PE bottoms, comes over. 'Emily,' she says. It's not a question.

'What?'

She's got Marianne with her, also in her bra and PE bottoms. They look like some bizarre pair of twins.

Lizzie doesn't seem to have planned the next part of

the conversation. She just stands there, looking at me.

Looking pointedly at my arms.

A cold fear washes over me. Why's she looking at me like that? I turn away, but they must have seen the anxiety on my face because Marianne whispers something to Lizzie, and Lizzie laughs.

'Show us your arms, Emily.'

'What?'

The world slows down. Other girls are starting to look at us.

'Show us your arms.'

I stare at them. 'What are you on, Lizzie? What have my arms got to do with you?'

'We're just curious,' says Marianne. 'We want to know why you wouldn't take your jumper off.'

'Why you won't take it off now,' adds Lizzie.

Oh my God. I look around helplessly, but there is nowhere to go. 'It's none of your business,' I say sharply, and I pick up my bag. I'll have to get changed later. I need to get out now.

But Marianne has moved like lightning and she's blocking the way out.

'Oh, leave her alone,' says Maia.

'We're not doing anything,' says Marianne, eyes flashing. 'We just wondered if there was something we should know.'

'Something we should all know,' says Lizzie.

Every single girl in the cloakroom is looking at us. I can feel the tension in the air. It is making me feel sick.

I decide to try to bluff my way out. 'You're all crazy,'

I say, and I take three steps towards the door.

But Marianne grabs me by the shoulders and I wince. The dressing shifts again under my clothes. 'Oh no, I don't think you're going anywhere just yet,' she says silkily. She pushes me back against the wall. 'If you won't show us your arms, we'll just have to have a look ourselves, won't we?'

Lizzie steps forward, smirking.

I start to struggle. But there is no escape. It crosses my mind to scream, but what for? Who would help me?

Lizzie and Marianne's hands are grabbing me by the arms and I am kicking, swearing at them, as the strap on my schoolbag breaks and my books fall to the floor, being trampled under my feet and theirs. Pens and pencils spill out in a multicoloured cascade as Marianne wrenches up the sleeve of my jumper.

'Holy Christ.'

I will never forget their faces. Shock, yes. Pity, from some. But from all – disgust. It crossed their faces like a bad smell.

And the silence. Total evaporation of sound, apart from a collective gasp from the other girls.

'Fucking hell . . .' Lizzie said, staring at the red, pink and white lines that criss-crossed my arm. Then she looked at me, and the hatred and repulsion that burned in her eyes made me dizzy.

'My God,' Marianne said, after what felt like hours. 'You're even more fucked up than I thought.' She dropped my arm as though it were diseased, and backed away. 'You are sick, Emily Bowyer. Sick and pathetic.'

Then they walked away, leaving me sobbing on the floor.

Lizzie and Marianne go straight to Miss Jarrow. After twenty minutes of sitting on the floor alone, I hear foot-steps on the lino.

'Emily Bowyer.'

I lift my head. Her voice has been sharp, but her face softens somewhat as she looks at me. 'Come along,' she says gently. 'I think we need to have a talk.'

I have no energy left, nothing to fight with any more. Everyone knows now. My life will not be worth living from now on. Everywhere I go, girls will look at me and whisper. They do it now, on the way to her office.

'Sit down.'

She closes the door firmly and takes her place behind the desk. 'Now, two girls have come to me with some very worrying news, and I'm afraid I have to ask for your side of the story.'

I gaze blankly at the paperweight in the shape of a hippo on her desk. It is not weighing down any paper.

'Emily, I am afraid that I have to ask you to show me your arms.'

I glance up in horror.

'Now.'

A cold, sick feeling washes over me. Obediently, I roll up my sleeves.

There is a sharp intake of breath. I daren't look up. I simply carry on staring at the hippo.

'I see,' she says eventually, although her voice wobbles a bit. 'And am I to assume that you have been doing this to yourself? That you made those – marks?'

I nod at the hippo.

'I suppose you got the idea from Patrice Evans,' she says.

I look up. 'What? No, I didn't.'

'Patrice has been through a tough time, Emily,' she says. 'There are problems at home. And whilst we have all been as sympathetic as we can, I really don't see that you need copy this destructive behaviour.'

'She copied me!' I burst out.

Miss Jarrow looks at me, one eyebrow raised.

'You don't believe me,' I say.

'It's not that, Emily. I just don't see why you would be doing this sort of thing. Patrice has been through some very unpleasant times, whilst you – what reason have you got?' She looks at me hard. 'Why are you doing this to yourself too?'

There is nothing I can say. Nothing that she will believe anyway.

'Your brother has learning difficulties, doesn't he?' she says, her voice dropping again.

'What has that got to do with anything?' It comes out more rudely than I intended.

She leans forward and crosses her hands on the desk. 'Are you doing this for attention, Emily? Is that what it is? Are you doing this because your brother has had a lot of extra help?'

'*What*? Are you completely mad?' I am furious now.

'Of course I'm not doing this for attention! If I was, do you think I'd be walking around with my arms covered up all the time?'

'That's enough,' she says crisply. Then she reaches for the telephone. 'I am calling your parents to come and pick you up. Go and sit outside the door.'

When Mum arrives, Miss Jarrow takes her into the office without me. I expect she thinks Mum doesn't know. For the first time, I feel grateful that Mum has already found out. I don't know what I'd do if the first she'd heard was from my teacher.

They are not in there very long, but when Mum comes out she is white. 'I think you'd better come in,' she says.

Miss Jarrow is looking slightly less frosty. 'I understand that you are having counselling, Emily. I think that is a very good idea. I have suggested to your mother that a short period away from school might be beneficial, both for you and the other girls in your class.'

'But what about my GCSEs?' I say in horror.

'There's nothing to stop you studying at home, Emily,' Miss Jarrow says sternly. 'Most of your coursework is out of the way now, and it is just a question of revising what you have already covered.'

'Miss Jarrow thinks,' says Mum, in a tone of voice that suggests she doesn't agree, 'that it would be useful for you to have some time out. The school is aware that you have had some problems with friends.'

'The question is,' says Miss Jarrow, 'what to do now. I suggest a week off from school. Emily's teachers will set homework and she can study at home. It will give her a little time to get things in perspective. You do understand,' she says to Mum, 'that we can't have this sort of thing going on in school.'

Mum glares. 'Really? Emily's managed to keep it a secret for several months, it seems. Are you sure there aren't others in the same position?'

Miss Jarrow coughs. 'As I am sure you know, Mrs Bowyer, this school does have a very comprehensive pastoral system. There is very little that goes on here that I don't know about.'

I cannot help myself. I am so wound up, I can't possibly hold back the laughter. She simply has no idea!

'Emily,' snaps my mother, but I can't stop. I laugh and laugh until I am not sure whether I am laughing or crying. Miss Jarrow stares at me in distaste, and over my laughter she says, 'I am sure we both agree, Mrs Bowyer, that Emily needs to reassess her priorities, and that the best place for her to do that is at home.'

So that's it. I am effectively suspended.

I don't really give a monkey's, to be honest. I feel as though I should, but I can't bring myself to muster up any kind of anger or disappointment about it. Everyone seems to care so much – why should I care too? There's enough energy being wasted already.

'Emily's been sent home from school,' Mum tells Dad

when he gets home. 'For a week.'

Anthony, watching television, looks up.

'Sent home? What for? Did she swear at a teacher?'

Anthony has saved Dad from having to answer. Dad's eyes flicker towards me, but he doesn't look at my face. 'I see,' he says.

I feel a burning anger. 'Is that all you can say?' I step forward.

'Emily.' Mum puts out a hand.

'No, I want to know what he thinks. What do you think, Dad? Because you've hardly spoken to me recently. Tell me. Do I disgust you? That's how you treat me.' My voice has taken on a sharp edge, and his shifty movements just make me angrier. 'Come on, talk to me. You can't even look at me any more, can you? Can't even look me in the face. As though I've suddenly turned into a completely different person! I'm your *daughter*. Look at me. *Look at me!*'

I have ended up right in front of his face, and he *still* won't raise his eyes.

'*That's enough!*' shouts Mum. She pulls me away. 'Don't you think you've caused enough trouble? You really think this is going to help?'

I stare at her, tears starting in my eyes. I thought she was on my side! She certainly was, in Miss Jarrow's office. Typical – I should never have expected her to sympathise. 'Help?' I snarl at her. 'Well, no. But then, *he's* not doing anything to help either, is he? Why aren't you shouting at him?'

'Stop it, all of you!' cries Anthony. He's kneeling on

the back of the sofa, tears streaming down his face. 'Stop shouting!'

Mum goes straight to Anthony. Dad goes straight to the kitchen.

I go straight to the piece of broken glass under my mattress.

a patch where there isn't any fog

'Tell me about your father.'

'I think he hates me.'

'Why do you think that?'

'He never talks to me any more. He won't even look at me. Ever since he found out –' I stop.

'Found out?'

I squirm. Here it comes. And it's funny, but now that I'm about to say it, I feel really embarrassed. Like it's something really shameful. I don't want David to know – which is silly, because he knows anyway; that's why I was sent here. But I suppose I'm worried it'll make him think less of me or something. What is the matter with my brain? 'Found out I've been – cutting myself.'

There. I said it.

'So when your father found out – he withdrew from you.'

I glance up quickly. Doesn't he want to talk about the cutting? 'Yes.'

'You used to be able to talk to him more freely.'

219

'Yes. He was always on my side. He used to let me do things Mum wouldn't. We had a laugh.'

'So you feel as though you've lost something. Something that used to be there with him. He doesn't talk to you and you don't talk to him.'

'I guess.'

'You feel as though you're on your own, but still – intruded upon. By your mother.'

'She's always there, but I can't talk to her properly. She just gets angry or upset. She's always following me around – she won't let me be in my room by myself.'

'Why is that?'

'Because she knows that's where –' I stop again. God, this is hard. 'That's where I keep my – things.'

'Your things.'

'My – my razor blades.' It sounds so stupid!

'Your razor blades. It seems as though you find it difficult to name them.'

'Well, I haven't talked about them with anyone before.'

David nods, but he doesn't say anything.

'And it makes them sound really bad if I call them that – but they're not bad. They help.'

'How do they help?'

'They make me feel better. Well, mostly. There was one time they didn't. They didn't work. And I got really worried. But the next time it was OK.' I still feel a chill when I think back to the night Patrice found out. I thought then that maybe I'd taken away the power – that the blades would never work again for me.

'When you say that they didn't work, I wonder what you mean by that?'

'I didn't feel better. Normally I feel – calmer.'

'Can you tell me a little bit about your feelings before you cut yourself? And then about the feelings when you cut yourself, and the feelings after you've cut yourself?'

It's almost as if this is a normal conversation. It doesn't feel quite so weird any more. And actually, it's quite nice to be able to tell someone. He's not reacting the way I expected. But I guess he hears this sort of thing every day, doesn't he? Something in me doesn't like that. It makes me sound like any other sort of messed-up teenager. And I'm not.

'Before, I feel . . . it's not always the same. I mean, sometimes I feel really angry, or sometimes I'm really tired. Or sometimes – you know that feeling you get when there's just too much going on in your head and it's like a thousand voices shouting at once and you can't hear yourself think?'

'So the feelings are always intense, even if they're not the same feelings.'

'Yes. And then . . . when I – cut, it's like they all go away.'

'Can you tell me how?'

Well, no, not really. I can't explain it myself. Everything is better somehow. I screw up my face, trying to think how to describe it. 'You know how when you're driving through fog, and you can't see anything and you don't know where you are. And then suddenly you come out into a patch where there isn't any fog – it's gone from completely white to no fog at all – and you can see again, and you think to yourself, ah, I know where I am now. It's like that.'

'Everything becomes clearer.'

'Yes. And I can think again. I can do what I have to do, and it's not so hard.'

'You can see your way again.'

'Yes. I can think properly. Mum's always said I think too much. I think a lot. But usually I think in straight lines. You know, I see a problem, I can think my way out of it, that kind of thing. But when I get really – wound up, I can't think logically. And I get really – scared. Well, not scared, but I can't think, and it's awful. And I just want it to go away.'

David nods. 'Do any thoughts come into your mind when you cut yourself?'

I frown. 'Not really. It's more like the thoughts go away.' I try to think back to last night. Did I think about anything then? 'I like how it looks,' I say suddenly, surprising myself. Now he really is going to think I'm weird. Why did I say that?

'How it looks.'

'Mmm. I like – the colour.' Suddenly the absurdity of the whole conversation is too much. 'And then I know I've got problems!' I feel the craziest urge to laugh. 'Because normal people don't do that, do they? So I must be really messed up. I must have real problems, mustn't I? Not just problems in my head. It's real. I can see my problems. They're there, on my arm.'

'And they're part of you. They're yours.'

'Yes. They're mine.'

A week off school is quite good really. I don't have to see Lizzie and Marianne and the other girls.

But in my head I can still see them.

Mum takes a week off work. She can't really afford it – I know because I hear her discussing it with Dad. But she doesn't want to leave me on my own.

As I lie in bed that night it suddenly crosses my mind that perhaps she thinks I'm going to try to kill myself.

February passes into March without my even noticing. Time is doing something strange. Some days seem to crawl by so slowly I can't believe the clocks haven't stopped. And other days I can't remember at all – they must have gone so quickly I didn't even notice them.

Mum sits me down after the suspension week and tries to get me to talk to her. But I just don't know what to say.

'Are you happy to go back to school?'

No. But I'm not happy to stay here either. But then 'happy' is surely the wrong word. I don't know how to answer, so instead I shrug.

Mum sighs. 'Emily, you have to make a decision about this. I can't stay off work for ever. You've got exams to take.'

I stare at the table. 'Sounds like I don't have any decision to make. You've already decided.'

She makes a noise of frustration. 'For God's sake,

Emily, we're trying to *help* you. How can we possibly guess what you want if you don't tell us?'

I don't say anything.

'I'm really at my wits' end with you. Since the counselling started you've been moodier and ruder than ever. What's got into you? Why can't you just pull yourself together and make a bit of an effort?'

I shrug.

'Don't just shrug, talk to me! For Christ's sake, Emily!' She stands up and glares at me. 'Right, that's it. You're going back to school. You're obviously not capable of making any sort of decision.'

'So why did you ask me, then?'

For a moment I think she's going to hit me. Then she turns and walks away, catching her jumper on the doorframe and pulling a long thread. 'Shit!'

I have never heard my mother swear before. I would laugh if it weren't so sad.

a homicidal maniac

I don't really know how I get through the rest of the term, but somehow it's not important. Every day, people stare at me in the corridors. The whole school knows now. Once or twice, girls try to get me to show them my arms. I take to wearing tight long-sleeved tops under my shirt so that they can't be pulled up easily. It has the added advantage of holding the dressings in place, of course.

Maia stops speaking to me again. I try not to mind, but inside I do. She was the only friendly face around. Now even she looks at me as though I have some sort of disease. In Biology we are supposed to dissect something. The teacher won't give me a scalpel. 'Oh dear, it looks like we've run out,' she says when I reach the front desk. 'Sorry.' But I see another box of scalpels in the cupboard, and so does Maia. She looks at me, but there's no sympathy in her gaze.

'Just as well,' I hear someone whisper. 'She'd probably slice our arms up too.'

So now I am a homicidal maniac as well.

Could life get any worse?

when it's a member of
your own family

School draws to its stupid, pointless close at Easter. I have seen David six times now but nothing has changed.

'Why am I here?' I ask him one session. 'What is the point? How can you help me?'

'I can't,' he says.

'What?'

'I can't help you. I can only help you to help yourself.'

What kind of bullshit is that?

'At the end of the day, you have to find a way through this yourself. I am here to help you find the way.'

I don't say it, but it sounds like a load of crap to me. All he has to do is sit there in his chair and listen. And then people go away and he still gets paid. What a jammy job.

A terrible disappointment washes over me. I thought he was going to help – solve my problems, make it all better. Now it turns out he's not going to do that at all. Or he can't. Even he doesn't know how to help me.

One really nice thing happens over Easter. Patrice comes round. I haven't seen her since she left school, and I haven't dared go round to her house again. The thought of meeting her brother again scares me.

I'm in my room, pretending to study (with the door open), when the doorbell rings.

'Emily, it's for you!' calls Mum. I hear her say 'Go right up' to the visitor.

For one glorious, heart-stopping minute, I think it might be Lizzie. She's come back – she's come to apologise for everything and to ask if she can be my friend again. She's come to say she's dropped Marianne, because she's realised what a total bitch she is.

When Patrice pokes her head round the doorway, I nearly cry. But I paint a welcoming smile on my face instead. 'Hi! How are you?'

Patrice looks happier than she has for ages. And not so white and frightened. 'Is it all right to come in? Are you revising?'

'Of course I'm not revising. I'm just staring at bits of paper. Come in. It's nice to see you.' And I do mean that.

She comes in and sits on the bed. 'I thought – I wanted to come and see you. To tell you what's been going on.'

'You don't have to.'

'No, I want to. You were really nice to me – the only one that was. And I'm going away soon so I won't get another chance.'

'Where are you going?'

She smiles suddenly, and I feel shocked. I'm not sure

I've ever seen her smile before. It's weird; her whole face changes. 'To live with my aunt and her boyfriend. In Chester.'

'Chester?' I don't even know where that is.

'Yeah. They've offered to look after me for a year. I'm going to take my GCSEs up there at a college. They said I don't have to take any, but I want to. I'm only taking five, though. Then I can stay on at the college and do some more next year.'

It sounds like bliss to me – spreading the stupid exams out so they don't all come at once. I nearly say, 'Can I come?' but I manage not to. 'What about your – um?'

'My brother?' Her face hardens slightly. 'He's been charged by the police. Mum threw him out and he came back one night and smashed all the windows.'

'Oh my God.'

'We hid in the back room and Mum called the police. She said she wasn't taking it any more.'

'Why didn't she do that years ago?'

Patrice shrugged. 'Oh, you know – it's hard, isn't it, when it's a member of your own family?'

Doesn't seem hard to me, but I hold my tongue.

'She felt guilty, I think. Like it was her fault in some way.'

'So what happened?'

'The police came and arrested him. They took him to a station.'

'What about your mum?'

Patrice looks at the floor. 'She went a bit – she kind

228

of lost it. Crying for days. She had some sort of break-down, I think.'

'So where is she?'

'Staying with a friend. She's got to be kept quiet, they said. Darkened rooms and all that. So I couldn't stay with her.'

I look at her. 'Don't you mind?'

She looks back at me for a long moment. 'You won't tell anyone this, will you?'

'No, of course not.'

She takes a deep breath. 'I don't mind at all. I thought I would, but I don't. She wasn't ever there for me. She never backed me up. She was just really – weak. I always had to be the strong one. Now I don't have to. She can't depend on me now. I get to have my own life at last. I don't miss her at all. In fact, I prefer not having her around.' She stops. 'Do you think I'm a bad person?'

'No, course I don't.' But I can't imagine feeling that way about my mum. I mean, sometimes I hate her guts, but I can't imagine being pleased that she's left. 'So when do you go?'

'Next Tuesday. My aunt's staying with me at the moment and helping me get the house sorted. The police said they might need me to come back at some point and be a witness at the trial.'

She says this so coolly. It sounds terrifying to me, but then I guess she's been living with much worse for ages. 'Wow,' I say.

'Yeah.'

There's a pause.

'So how are you?' she says finally.

I stare at her. I don't really know what to say. 'All right.'

She nods. 'How's school?'

'Boring.'

She grins. 'Right.' Her gaze flicks down to my arms and I can see she's trying to work out whether to say something or not. 'So is everything – all right now?'

'Not everything,' I say. 'But I'm seeing someone. To talk to.'

Her eyes widen. 'What, a therapist?'

'A counsellor,' I correct her.

'Wow. What's that like?'

I shrug. 'OK. A bit weird to start with, but he's really nice.'

'He?' She shudders. 'I don't think I could talk to a man.'

'Neither did I, but he's all right actually.'

'Is he – helping?'

I frown. 'Not really. I mean, it's kind of nice to talk, but I don't really feel I'm getting anywhere.'

'I guess it takes time,' she says wisely. 'Some people are in therapy for years, aren't they?'

This is a horrifying thought. Years? I hadn't banked on that. 'Oh, I don't suppose it'll be for much longer,' I say with an attempt at a laugh. 'Once he's realised there's no hope for me he'll give up. I'm a lost cause.'

She laughs with me.

When Patrice has gone, I take down my box. Mum has

been in touch with David. I don't like her talking to him, but he's giving her good advice. He told her that it is better for me to be using sterile equipment and looking after myself properly than have to resort to using slicers from the food processor. So I have been allowed my blades again. She doesn't like it, but there's nothing she can do. David told her that if I wanted to hurt myself I would find a way to do it. I think she already knew that, but he persuaded her that I should be allowed my blades again.

I take out the blade automatically. I roll up my sleeve and look for a place.

But then I stop. I am thinking about Patrice. She seems so much happier. She has been through so much, such terrible things. If she can be happy, might it work for me again? Could things go back to the way they were?

But Patrice was being hurt by other people. Her family life was awful. Nobody cared about her; nobody was looking out for her. Things are better for her now because her brother has been taken away and she is being given a new start.

It's different for me. I don't have all those awful things in my past. I can't work out why I've started to do this. It's not other people who are to blame; it's me. My life was – is – fine, compared with hers. It's all in my head, isn't it?

I raise the blade again.

'Emily! Dinner!'

I freeze, the blade poised above my arm. I can't do it

now. The cleaning up takes too long.

I put the blade back in the box. I can do it later, I reason. After dinner.

'So did you do it after dinner?' David asks.

I frown. 'No. I forgot.'

'You forgot.'

'Well – not exactly forgot. But I couldn't be bothered.'

'You didn't feel bad enough?'

'I suppose.'

'Tell me about after you cut. What do you do?'

'I clean it up. I make sure it's clean.' I look at him defensively. Is he suggesting I can't look after myself? 'I don't get infections, you know.'

'Tell me what you do.'

'Well, I put the blade down on some tissues and then I hold more tissues to the cut. I sit like that for a few minutes. Then . . .' I screw up my forehead, trying to think. 'Then I lift the tissues off and look at the cut. If it's still bleeding, I press down again with the tissues. Sometimes I poke it a bit.'

'You poke it?'

'Yes. To make it bleed a bit more.' I squirm. God, I sound so morbid. 'Then, when it's stopped bleeding, I wipe away the blood. Sometimes I go to the bathroom and run it under the tap. Then I dry it off. And I stick a dressing over it.'

'A dressing?'

'Yeah, with tape. I've got some ready-prepared dressings in different sizes. But usually I get the same size.'

'Because the cuts are usually a certain size?'

'Yes. Although sometimes they're deeper than other times.'

'But you like cleaning up?'

'Yes. I like – looking after myself.'

'Why do you think that is?'

I hesitate. 'I don't know. Maybe it's – it's something I can do all on my own. I know how to do it. I do it right. It doesn't involve anyone else. It's mine – I control it.'

David smiles slightly and nods.

Bizarrely, I have this strange feeling he's pleased with me.

Even more bizarrely, his being pleased with me makes me feel good.

some people might say that you are craving attention

I don't know when I decide that going to see David is actually a good thing. I haven't really cared about it up to now, but since the cleaning-up conversation, I've actually found myself looking forward to going. I save up things to tell him. I even think to myself, *I must tell David that*, when something strange or weird or funny happens.

For the first time, I have someone to talk to who won't tell me their own problems. David listens to me. I don't have to listen to him. He's paid to sit there and listen to me. It's brilliant.

Of course, there are times when he makes me mad. On one occasion, he wants me to talk about the exams.

'Tell me how you feel about the GCSEs.'

I shrug. 'Don't care.'

'You don't care whether you do well or not?'

'Doesn't seem much point any more.'

'Don't you think you're taking the easy way out?'

I glance up. 'What do you mean?'

'You think it'll be easier not to care, so you pretend

234

you don't. Then you don't have to put pressure on your-self to do well.'

'What?' I stare. 'The easy way out? Easier not to care? Have you any idea how the teachers at school are nag-ging me?'

'But if you say you don't care, then you don't have to take responsibility.'

'Aren't you listening? I don't care. Read my lips: I-do-not-care. I don't. I've given up caring. Nothing I do or say makes any difference – it doesn't matter how much work I put in or not.'

'You feel you have no control?'

'Exactly.'

'And so you pretend you can't change things.'

'No – you're twisting what I'm saying! I *can't* change things. It doesn't matter how much work I do or don't do – I didn't work for the mocks, and I did fine. They weren't As but they were OK.'

'So you are deliberately trying to do badly this time. So that everyone will know you are hurting.'

I glare at him. 'You think I'm deliberately ruining my own chances of university and A Levels and all that?'

He raises his eyebrows. 'Aren't you?'

'No!' I almost shout. 'I just don't see the point, that's all! If I work, I do well, but it's never good enough! If I don't work, I still do fine – good enough for anyone else's parents anyway! Why should I have to get As – why can't I just be like everyone else?'

'You want to be like everyone else?'

'Oh, what's the point? You're not even listening to

me.' I thrust the sleeves of my jumper up to the elbow. 'This isn't normal, is it? Other people don't do this to themselves, do they?'

'Actually, they do.'

'What?'

'There are a lot of young people who self-harm. You would be surprised how many. It is a growing problem.'

I am speechless. It feels like he has just pulled the rug from under me. I pull my sleeves back down. 'You're saying I don't have any reason to be doing this.'

'No, not at all.'

'Yes, you are. You think I'm just doing this for attention, don't you?'

'Are you?'

I feel sick. After all I've told him, after pouring out my thoughts and my feelings to him, he thinks I'm just a stupid teenager trying to rebel.

David leans forward. 'Some people might say that you're jealous of your younger brother. Some people might say that because he's had all the attention and sympathy, you have resented his learning difficulties. He has taken up your parents' time and care. Your friends weren't interested in your problems, and when you started to demand that they listen, they left you. Some people might say that you are craving attention; for people to look at you and listen to you. And so you cut your arms so that people will see and feel sorry for you and will want to help you.'

There is a red-hot rage bubbling up inside me.

How dare he say these things! I thought he was my friend, on my side!

'This isn't really about exam pressure at all, is it?'

'*Shut up, shut up!* You don't know anything – *how* can you –' I am so angry I can barely speak. 'It's got nothing to do with Anthony! *Nothing!* He's my brother, I've never resented him! You have absolutely *no* idea what I've been going through! These exams are huge – everyone's always going on about them, like your life won't be worth living if you don't pass them! You can't get away from them – at school, at home – everywhere I go people tell me I am clever, big things are expected. Have you any idea what it's like to hear that all the time? Have you *any idea* what it's like living with my *fucking mother?*'

I stop suddenly, out of breath and tearful.

David nods, but he doesn't say anything.

'I didn't mean to swear. I don't usually.'

'That's all right. You don't have to apologise.'

'I didn't mean to shout at you either.'

'Do you feel better now? Having shouted at me?'

Do I feel better? I don't know. It was quite good to really yell – I don't remember the last time I did that. A sudden suspicion crosses my mind. 'Did you do that on purpose?'

'Do what?'

'Make me shout at you?'

'What makes you think that?'

'I don't know.' I am doubtful again. Why would he make me shout at him anyway? I must be imagining things.

'Do you often feel angry?'

I have to think about this one. 'I guess so. Well, not really angry – more sort of annoyed. Frustrated.'

'Frustrated.'

'But not really *angry* angry – not like shouting-at-people angry.'

'Can you talk to people about feeling frustrated?'

'No.'

He nods.

It's funny, but ever since that evening when I couldn't cut because it was dinner-time, and I forgot to do it afterwards, I've been thinking about it a lot more. About how I feel and whether I could stop.

That's a scary thought. I don't want to stop, don't get me wrong. I'm just wondering if I could. If I wanted to.

I experiment a couple of times. When the blade is poised over my arm, I hesitate. I look at the clock. I count a whole minute. There. I've proved I don't *have* to do it.

But I *want* to do it. So I go on and cut anyway.

But I've proved I could stop. If I wanted to.

bolognese

I'm making bolognese sauce for dinner. One of Mum's new ideas: 'keep her busy, don't let her think about anything else.' Because, of course, if you're cooking the dinner you can't possibly think at the same time.

I'm chopping onions with the kitchen knife. On the gas ring, the frying pan is sizzling with hot oil. The onions are slippery and I have to hold them down firmly so they don't slide off the chopping board.

I don't realise Mum's there until I turn to put the chopped onions in the pan. 'Jesus, Mum, what are you trying to do – give me a heart attack?'

She's staring at my hands. I look down and see the shiny, sharp knife. Her face changes in a second, but I've seen how she feels. She thinks I'm going to do it here, right here, doesn't she? In front of her! She smiles, too quickly.

'How are you getting on?'

'Fine.' I can't think of anything else to say. 'Just fine.'

'Do you need any help?'

'No.' I turn back to the board and pick up the next

onion. I can tell she hasn't gone; I can feel her eyes on my back.

Yasmine said she once did this experiment with tinfoil. You cut out a piece of tinfoil and fold it into a small square. Then you stick it to your back. You walk around with it on the whole day and when you take it off at night it's got all these little holes in it. 'So you can see how many people have been stabbing you in the back all day,' Yasmine said. 'There was one really deep hole that had gone right through all the layers. I reckon that's when my stepdad told me off for eating the last of the KitKats and not writing it on the list. I could feel his eyes burning into my back as I walked away.'

If I were wearing tinfoil on my back right now, my mum's eyes would not just be boring through it; they would be destroying it utterly, shrivelling it to ashes. Knowing she's looking at me makes me nervous, and I accidentally lose my grip on the slippery onion. The knife jerks sideways and slices into my thumb. I exclaim in shock and run my thumb under the tap. The cut isn't deep, but thumbs bleed an awful lot. I watch the red drops mix with the water as it swirls down the plughole. It stings from the onion juice.

Mum has come over, and is reaching for my hand. 'Let me see.'

I pull away. 'It's fine. It's just a cut.' Maybe I speak more sharply than I meant, because her face hardens.

'Well, are you happy now?'

'What?' I stare at her.

'Are you happy?' she repeats, as though I'm deaf. 'You cut yourself. Are you happy?'

Something inside me goes cold. 'I didn't do it on purpose.'

'Are you sure?' Her face is right in mine, twisted. 'Maybe you did it unconsciously. Maybe you wanted to.'

'It was an accident,' I say shakily. This is nothing like when I cut myself in my room. That's private; it's my moment. 'How can you think –?'

She stares at me for a moment, but although she opens her mouth to speak, nothing comes out. At least, I don't think it does. But it's as if I've missed a minute or two of real time, because she suddenly crumples, the corners of her eyes creasing. As though somebody's just let the air out of her. She lets out this funny sound and runs out of the room, her hand over her mouth.

I don't understand how we got to that. She was mad at me, and then suddenly she was really upset. How did that happen? My mind feels foggy, still reeling from the idea that she thinks I stuck the kitchen knife into my thumb on purpose. Maybe my mind went elsewhere for a moment, and when it came back it didn't know what to do. Was I supposed to say something?

I am dripping blood on the floor. I reach for the kitchen towel and wrap a piece around my thumb. Then I get down on the floor and mop up the drips.

The onions in the pan have fried themselves to blackness. I turn the gas off and throw them in the bin. Then I sit at the table and stare at my paper-towelled thumb. After a while, I unwrap it to look at the cut. It's about a centimetre long and it's stopped bleeding. I prod it, trying to see how deep it is. If I squeeze the ends of it, it opens up, like one of those paper games you can make where you have to choose numbers or colours and it tells you something stupid under one of the flaps – 'You have ten boyfriends,' that sort of thing. We used to make them at primary school.

I squeeze the cut as hard as I can, and the blood starts to well up again. I make bloody thumbprints on the kitchen towel. How many would I be able to make before I ran out of blood? I bet I could make millions – there's about eight pints in my body, right? And one thumbprint would only use a tiny amount. I pat my thumb round in circles. It looks like a ring of roses. Ring-a-ring-a-roses . . .

I don't know how long I sit there, but when Dad gets back from work, there's no dinner and he has to go back out for fish and chips. He's really cross. Mum's been crying again and Ant is sitting there looking very confused.

Why am I the only one in therapy?

things are different now

School is out! I can't believe I made it this far – I did bunk off a few days in the summer term, but it doesn't matter now because we're officially on study leave. I don't suppose I'll be going back for sixth form. Strangely, Mum agrees with me.

'I think it'd be best if you had a fresh start somewhere for A Levels,' she says cheerfully, not even contemplating the fact that I may not pass any exams. 'The college has a good reputation and although it's not what we'd have wanted for you, things are different now.'

Lizzie is planning to stay on at school. So is Marianne, surprise, surprise. Maia and Yasmine have sort of drifted away from them. Yasmine's stepdad has a new job in Spain and she thinks they're all moving out there. Maia doesn't really know what to do.

Of course, none of them tell me this. I overhear it in class. None of them bother to turn their backs on me any more. I am simply invisible.

Study leave is supposed to mean revision. I know this, but I can't seem to do it. I spend hours in my room playing with paper aeroplanes or making jewellery. Mum has encouraged my new hobby (she thinks it will 'take my mind off other things' like CUTTING), but she doesn't realise how long I spend making things instead of actually learning my French vocab or rereading my English texts.

I haven't cut on two occasions when I thought I would. It's been very strange. I even went so far as getting the box out and taking the lid off. But then I saw the unfinished necklace on the side, or heard the theme music of my favourite TV programme, and I changed my mind.

I am allowed to change my mind. It doesn't mean I want to stop.

David is very interested when I tell him this. 'Have you ever kept a diary?' he suggests. 'Have you tried writing poetry?'

'Instead of cutting?' I scoff. Like it's that easy.

'No, not instead of cutting. I just thought that perhaps, seeing as you're so artistic, you might try expressing some of your feelings through poetry or painting.'

This is an interesting idea. Part of me (quite a large part) thinks this is a load of crap, but I find myself digging out a blank notebook that someone gave me for Christmas (Why do aunts and grandmas do that? Why do they imagine I need so many blank notebooks or address books?) and scrawling some ideas in pencil. They are pretty crap, but once I start I can't really stop.

Trapped.
Why is everything so hard?
Red, I like red
Dripping down my arm
Encircling my life
Red is my life
It is love and life
My love is running out of me
Losing my life in the red.
Seasons change, but my life goes dully, redly, on
What is the point?
Why am I here?
Am I here to make others miserable?
Am I here to suffer?
Am I here to make myself suffer?
If not, why do I do it?
Why am I compelled to ruin my own life and love?
Perhaps there is something wrong
Deep down
Genetically
I cannot feel
Maybe I am lacking a chromosome
Or a gene
The happy gene.
I think I had it once
But I lost it
Someone took it away.

It's funny, but writing does actually help in a way. I mean, it's not as good as cutting, but I can look at my problems, see them on the page, like when I see the cuts on my arm. It makes them real.

David is pleased when I tell him this. 'Can you write about anger too? Can you express your frustration in words?'

I frown. 'It's harder. And it's not very – polite.' Absurdly, I blush. I have written some poems made up entirely of swearwords. If my mother knew, she'd kill me.

'Anger isn't polite,' says David. 'And often when we're angry, we want to use words that we know are normally forbidden. We want to use language that is stronger than usual because the feelings are stronger than usual. It makes sense really.'

'I guess.'

'Are you worried that your mother will find the book?'

'She hasn't been through my room lately. At least, I don't think she has. But I don't want her to see it.'

'I have suggested to your mother that she gives you some privacy.'

'Really?' I didn't know that. That would explain why she hasn't been in my room so much. She's even knocked on occasion – wonders will never cease!

'Your writing isn't for anyone else. It's just for *you*. Only *you* need to see it.'

'Do you want to see it?'

'Only if you want to show it to me.'

A moment ago, I would have completely rejected

any suggestion that I show it to him. Perversely, now he has said he's not bothered, I feel like I *want* to show him. Weird.

'Do you feel that you are being given a little more space at home?'

'Sometimes, yes. Mum doesn't follow me around so much.'

'What about your father?'

I screw up my nose. 'No change there. He talks to me when he has to, but he still doesn't like looking at me.'

'How does that make you feel?'

I feel upset suddenly. 'I'm getting used to it. I can't really remember what it was like before now. But it was only a couple of months ago. Can people really change that quickly?'

'Has he changed? As a person?'

'As a person? I don't know. Well – yeah, I guess he has. He used to be really happy and cheerful – make jokes, that kind of thing. He used to laugh a lot more than he does now.'

'How does he behave towards Anthony?'

'Anthony? The same, I think.'

'The same as before?'

'Well – actually, now I come to think of it, no, it isn't really the same. He doesn't really joke around with Anthony like he used to.'

'How does Anthony feel about that?'

'I don't know.' With a slight shock, I realise that I haven't really talked to my brother for weeks. He doesn't come and knock on my door any more, and I have no idea how he's doing at school. I don't even know what his new learning support assistant is like. 'We don't really talk any more.'

'You don't really talk?'

'No.'

I feel bad about this.

Later that evening, I go to Anthony's room. 'Hi,' I say.

Anthony looks up. He's sitting on his bed reading a book. This surprises me, since I know he hates reading. 'Hi.'

'Can I come in?'

He shrugs. 'Yeah.'

I sit next to him. 'What are you reading?'

'*Harry Potter.*'

'Wow. Is it good?'

'Yeah. Bit confusing, though.'

'Oh. Is it for school?'

'No.' He looks scornfully at me. 'Why would school want me to read *Harry Potter*?'

'I dunno. I didn't think you liked reading much. I thought school must have told you to.'

'I'm reading much better now,' Ant says shortly. 'I can read all sorts of stuff. Miss Sayid says I'm making great progress.'

'That's brilliant.'

There's a pause. I don't really know what to say next.

'Don't you like me any more, Emily?' Ant suddenly blurts out.

'What?'

'You haven't come to talk to me for ages. You never laugh at my jokes now – you never laugh at all, these days. Is it me? Have I done something?'

Oh God. How could he even think it is something *he* did? 'No,' I say. 'No, no, you mustn't think that. It's not you at all, Ant. It's me. Something happened.'

'What?'

'I don't really know. Lots of things went wrong. My friends stopped speaking to me. The teachers at school kept telling me to work harder. Mum kept telling me to work harder. I don't know.' Put like that, my reasons sound pathetic. 'I just got really upset with everything. I felt like nobody was listening to me. I wasn't in control of my own life. I just – wanted everything to be easier.'

'Is that why you cut your arms?'

I look at him in shock.

'Oh, don't be stupid, Emily, I've known for ages. It's pretty obvious really.'

'Obvious?'

'Yeah. I'm not thick, you know.'

'I know you're not. I'm sorry I didn't tell you.'

'That's OK. I don't tell you everything either. How does it help?'

'I don't know. It just does.'

He nods. 'You're not going to do it for ever, though, are you?'

'No, of course not.'

He nods again. 'Because that would be kind of dumb. Besides, you'd run out of room, wouldn't you?'

My little brother is the only one to put his finger on

the truth. It *would* be kind of dumb to do this for ever. And do I really want my entire body covered in scars for the rest of my life?

At that point, I decide that this has to end. Soon.

I am scared out of my wits.

imagining everything?

I soon realise that stopping may not be as easy as I thought. It's one thing to hold off doing it for a minute; it's quite another to not do it at all.

The first night is horrible. I go to my box as usual: it's habit – it's what I do, who I am. I take out the blade. And then I stop. Do I really have to do it tonight? Am I feeling bad enough? Nothing has happened to make me angry or upset. How do I feel?

It's horrible. Suddenly it's like my entire body is alien to me. I can't tell if I'm happy or sad – I can't read my own emotions at all. I no longer know how I feel. How can that be so? How can I have detached myself from my own feelings? Is that even possible? Is this another sign that I am going crazy? After all, I am seeing a psychotherapist – am I mentally ill? Or am I simply imagining everything?

The idea of not cutting is suddenly an impossible one. I cut because I need to know how I feel. And as the blade pierces my skin, the emotions come flooding back and I feel so relieved.

The euphoria lasts for about ten minutes. Then I look at the mess I have made of my arm and I burst into hot tears. I am such a failure.

day-to-day grind

The GCSE exams begin. It is strange to be back at school but for it to feel so different. The corridors are dominated by large signs saying QUIET - EXAMS and the students obsess over clear plastic pencil cases and whether their calculator works rather than over their hair or the weekend.

I know that I have not done enough revision. Even those students predicted D grades have probably done more than I have. I have done virtually nothing. It feels very odd, because normally I am panicking and desperately trying to remember facts in the last few minutes. But this time I am unusually calm. My stomach is empty because I have thrown up my breakfast before heading out. My body is obviously nervous, but my brain is not.

The first paper is Maths.

I don't do very well.

That night, I succeed in not cutting myself. This is partly because Anthony insists on the whole family sitting down and playing Monopoly, just like we used to. I try to claim that I have revision to do, but to my surprise Ant tells me I need a break and that anyway I don't have an exam the next day.

'You need some fun in your life,' he tells me firmly, and I think I catch a twinkle in Dad's eye, but I am not sure.

It is a laugh actually. Mum gets sent to Jail four times in the space of five minutes and Ant gets Mayfair and Park Lane the first time round the board. Naturally, he manages to bankrupt the rest of us. By the time we finish, it is late and I am yawning. Everyone's in a cheerful mood, and, unusually, nothing happens to spoil it. It's almost like old times. I go to my room, flick a glance at the hiding place for my box and take a book to bed instead.

In the morning I feel triumphant, but I know that it wasn't actually my will-power that prevented me from cutting.

GCSEs wear on and on. I don't know how, but the subjects I'm taking seem to be the most spread out. Lizzie finishes her exams a week before I do, and I hear her discussing a party with Marianne. They are going to hire a local outdoor pool and invite everyone from the year. Except me, of course. I mean, they don't actually say that, but I know I wouldn't be welcome.

I miss Patrice. I've had a couple of emails from her since she moved away, but I miss our bus journeys. And I miss the fact that she was the only one who came close to understanding. She's sent me the email address of someone she says was nice to her at school. It's a girl I only know by sight. Patrice says she's moving into my street and is really shy. I've sent a 'hello' kind of message but I haven't heard back. Maybe she's too shy even for emails.

The exams are hard. I don't mean the questions themselves – they're only hard because I haven't done enough revision – but simply the day-to-day grind. After a couple of two-hour papers I lose count of how many exams I have to do. I turn up at my French exam with my calculator. The invigilator, who's some History teacher I don't know, removes the calculator from my desk with a smirk. 'Don't think your calculator will help you work out the answers to this one.'

Har har har.

But they end at last, as they have to do. Oddly, I don't feel very relieved. I have been anxiously obsessing over GCSEs for so long that it feels strange not to have to worry any more. It's as though my mind is permanently on 'anxiety' level – how do I switch it off?

can we start again?

Mum takes me out for dinner – just me. I don't think she's ever done it before.

'I just thought it'd be nice to have some time with just us two,' she tells me.

'Right.'

It's a sweet little café place that serves pasta and big chocolatey puddings. 'Have whatever you like,' she says. So I choose a bowl of penne pasta with tomato, mozzarella and spicy sausage, followed by a chocolate gateau thing with lots of whipped cream. By the time we have finished I am totally stuffed.

Mum is chatty and cheerful. She even orders me a glass of wine. 'Well done,' she says at the end of the meal.

'Yes,' I pat my tummy. 'It was a tough job, but someone had to do it.'

'I mean about the exams.'

'Oh.' I look up, surprised.

'I just wanted to say –' Mum clears her throat nervously, '– that I'm really proud of you for getting through them.'

I am speechless.

'I know it's been a tough year for you, and I want you to know I'm really proud of you for hanging in there. And whatever the results are, we'll be happy.'

I find it difficult to hide my disbelief. Really? Whatever results I get, she'll be happy? I don't think so! I bet she won't be happy if I come out with no grades at all!

Mum sees my expression. 'I don't mean that we won't be disappointed if they're not as good as you can achieve,' she says quickly. 'But we know this has been a difficult time and we're just so pleased – just so relieved – that you're still with us at all.' Her voice chokes up and she has to fumble with her serviette for a moment.

'Still with you? What do you mean?'

She looks at me, and the naked vulnerability in her eyes is almost too much. 'I thought', she says in a whisper, 'that we might lose you at some point. You went so far into yourself – I thought you might never come back. I thought you might decide that life wasn't worth living any more.'

I don't know what to say, so I fiddle with the stem of my wine glass. There is an awkward pause.

'I'm sorry if it's all my fault,' she says eventually. 'I know you and I haven't always seen eye to eye. I suppose most teenagers go through this with their parents. I never meant to upset you, but I suppose what you want and what I want aren't always compatible. And sometimes you don't give me a chance to explain – and I know sometimes I haven't really listened to you either.'

'Mm.'

'I've been really scared,' she adds surprisingly. 'My mother was depressed for quite a while when I was growing up. I never really got to know her. She was always so difficult to talk to. I was determined that you and I should have a good relationship, that you should feel able to come and tell me anything. And when you – got depressed too, I thought it was all happening again. Maybe I smothered you a bit. I was just so worried you were going to shut me out. Like my mother did.'

Her voice wobbles and I don't know where to look. It certainly explains a lot.

'So I guess what I'm trying to say is – can we start again? I'm trying to be more sensitive to your needs, but I will make mistakes. I'm only human after all. But I think I understand a little bit more now about everything you've been going through. I can't pretend I understand about the – the cutting, but I am trying to. There's a lot of information on the internet, you know. I've been looking for websites and forums, and they've really helped me to see where you're coming from. And David has been so helpful too. I've rung him up on a number of occasions and asked him what I should do. I think things have been a little bit better recently, but I know it's going to take time. I just want you to know that I'm here for you – we both are. Your dad's found it very hard to understand about – everything. He had a terrible shock. And he's not very good at expressing his feelings. Perhaps you take after him.' She smiles slightly, and I find myself smiling back. 'But he'll come round. I hope you know that we're on your side – we'll always be on your side.'

She says this so simply that I believe her. And inside me, it's as though something has burst or melted. She's always going to push me. *I'm* always going to push me. But basically, she still loves me. Whatever I do. And that's amazing.

'So what did you say?' asks David.

'I didn't say anything,' I admit. 'I couldn't. I wanted to say loads but I didn't know how. I just sort of said, "Oh good, right," in a pathetic kind of way. She looked a bit disappointed. But she just sort of sprang it on me. I wasn't ready.'

'How did you feel when she told you all those things?'

'Really good,' I say slowly. 'I mean, she's never said anything like that before. Well – she sort of has, but it's always been along the lines of "you must do your best, you must do well" kind of thing. Not like that. Like she actually meant it.'

'Did you feel that you wanted to say something back? To respond?'

'Well, yeah. I mean, she was obviously pouring her heart out and all that. And I'm grateful, of course I am. For everything she said. It was – nice. But I didn't have time to think.'

'If you had some time to think, what might you say?'

I stare at the floor for a while. Then I look up. 'Thank you, I guess. I don't really know what else to say.'

'That sounds like a good start.'

smile

I haven't cut for two whole weeks now. That's incredi-
ble for me. But I know that I won't have to face Lizzie
or Marianne ever again. Or Miss Jarrow. And Patrice's
friend, Mandie, has emailed back. She sounds really
nice, and she says she's got a younger brother who drives
her crazy. Her email was really funny.

The GCSE results are due out next week. Mum says
that even if I fail half of them, I can retake them at the
college. She's being brilliant. She keeps having all these
ideas of things I could do. She got hold of the college
prospectus and keeps saying things like 'Ooh, have you
thought of doing a GNVQ or an HND in jewellery
making? There's a fascinating course here on silverwork
and semi-precious gems. Or aromatherapy? What about
art therapy?'

Actually, I quite like the sound of art therapy. It's using
art to express how you feel and working with people
who have various problems, like learning difficulties or
mental health problems. I'd need some more qualifica-
tions first, but Mum says I can stay at home for as long as

I need to. She's got so excited she's even signed up for a course herself – Indian Head Massage, whatever that is. And it turns out that Mandie's going to college too. So at least there'll be one friendly face there.

Dad's thawed out a bit. I sort of tried to talk to him and although it didn't go very well he's been a lot nicer to me since. I think he still finds it really hard to understand why I continue to cut my arms. This isn't surprising – I still find it hard to understand myself.

I haven't stopped cutting for ever. I haven't cut for two weeks but I know I will some time. It's not that easy just to give up something that gives your life meaning. Something that helps you to get through the day. David says that the urge will never go away completely. 'Whenever you are stressed in the future, it will occur to you as a possible way to deal with problems. But you will be that much stronger for having overcome it in the past. And now you have different ways of dealing with stress.'

'Yeah, I paint really bad pictures and write really bad poetry.'

'But if it helps you to express what is inside you – to make it real, give it validity – then it doesn't matter if it's bad. You could write the most beautiful poetry in the world and it wouldn't express what you are really feeling. The quality doesn't matter. What matters is that you are doing it instead of cutting yourself. That is what you need to remember.'

Every night, I look at my box. Sometimes I take it down and just hold it for a minute. Sometimes I even get as far as taking the lid off and looking at the contents. I know that some time in the near future I shall have to cut again. But I know now that it doesn't have to be every night. It doesn't even have to be every week. It's a long road, and the sad thing is that I won't ever be 'cured'. Sometimes I feel so sad that I ever started this, but at other times I know that I'm coming out of it a stronger person. It's almost as though I've found who I am. I know I can be stupid and clumsy, and that sometimes I can be over-anxious and too much of a perfectionist. But somehow I'm learning that that's OK. That's me. And I don't have to change me in order to be happy – or at least, not unhappy. And I don't have to beat myself up every time I get something wrong. Look how much I've got wrong over the last year. And cutting my arms hasn't made any of it better in the long run. It just papered over the cracks. Covered it all up so I wouldn't have to deal with the real problems.

Anthony said something that made me smile the other day. We were doing the washing-up together – I was washing and he was drying. I had to roll my sleeves up so they wouldn't get wet. My arms are covered with scars from shoulder to wrist. It makes me feel sad when I look at them. They are a reminder of all the times I've failed, it seems to me. But Anthony said, 'You know, it could be really useful having all those lines on your arm.'

'Useful?' I stared at him.

'Yeah. You could mark off the lines in centimetres, and it'd be like having your own personal ruler with you the whole time. I'm always forgetting mine.'

I laughed so much that Dad came in to see what all the noise was about. He frowned at us. 'Honestly, you two. Any excuse to get out of the washing-up. You'd better give me that cloth – you're obviously incapable of doing anything other than drip all over the floor.'

This was quite true, since I was so hysterical that my soapy hands were sending drips flying.

I can't remember when I last laughed like that.

It felt really good.

Joanna Kenrick was born in Oxfordshire and has a degree in Performing Arts from Middlesex University. She has worked as an actor, musician and singing teacher, and has run workshops for adults with learning disabilities. Joanna lives in Oxfordshire with her husband and teaches English and Drama at a secondary school. Her first book was published in 2004 and she says of *Red Tears*, 'Researching the book has actually made me more compassionate as a person and has helped me to be more sympathetic towards people with depression.'

Childline is a free helpline for children and young people in the UK. You can find it online at:
www.childline.org.uk or on the telephone: 0800 1111

Self-harm is not limited to young people. If you are an adult who would like help or information, please call the Samaritans on 08457 909090

You can find more information about self-harm and where to get help at: www.red-tears.com